STRUCK
BY
LIGHTNING

THE CARSON PHILLIPS JOURNAL

STRUCK
BY
LIGHTNING

THE CARSON PHILLIPS JOURNAL

Chris Colfer

**LITTLE, BROWN
AND COMPANY**

NEW YORK
BOSTON

Copyright © 2012 by Christopher Colfer
All photographs by Suzanne Houchin, courtesy of Camellia Entertainment

Little, Brown and Company

Hachette Book Group
237 Park Avenue, New York, NY 10017
Visit our website at www.lb-teens.com

Little, Brown and Company is a division of Hachette Book Group, Inc.
The Little, Brown name and logo are trademarks of
Hachette Book Group, Inc.

The publisher is not responsible for websites (or their content)
that are not owned by the publisher.

First Edition: November 2012

ISBN 978-0-316-23295-1

10 9 8 7 6 5 4 3 2 1

RRD-C

Printed in the United States of America

To Melissa Schwolow, Mikendra McCoy, Jenny Herrick, and Maureen Bagdasarian, without whom I would have never survived my own high school experience.

And to every president or captain of a writers' club, drama club, speech and debate team, Destination ImagiNation team, every editor of a high school newspaper or literary magazine, and anyone overachieving in their own right and underappreciated for it...this book is for you!

Dear Journal,

One more school year with these shitheads and I'll be free. It's taken almost two decades of careful planning, but I'm proud to say my overdue departure from the town of Clover is only *days* away. Three hundred and forty-five days away, to be exact, but who's counting?

A year from now I'll be sitting in my dorm room at Northwestern University taking notes from some overpriced textbook about "the history of...," you know, something historical. I'll be living off Top Ramen and gallons of Red Bull. I'll barely be getting five hours of sleep a night, and that's only when I don't have to yell at my roommate to turn down his porn.

I know it doesn't sound like much to look forward to, but for this college-bound kid, it's *paradise*! All the suffering, now and later, is for a much bigger picture.

It's not much of a secret since I tell anyone who will listen (mostly to get them to stop talking to me), but one day I hope to become the youngest freelance

1

journalist to be published in the *New York Times*, the *Los Angeles Times*, the *Chicago Tribune*, and the *Boston Globe*, eventually making my way to editor of the *New Yorker*.

Yes, I know that was a lot of information, so take a minute if you need one. If it sounds overwhelming to you, just think about how I feel living up to my future self every day. It's exhausting!

In a decade, if all goes according to plan, things will be much better for me. I can see it now: I'll be sitting in my New York City apartment applying final touches to my weekly *New York Times* column. I'll be living off Thai food and bottles of the finest red wine. I'll be sleeping ten hours a night, even when I have to yell at my neighbor to turn down his porn.

Granted, I still have a year to go in high school, and *senior* year at that. And I do realize I haven't actually been "accepted" to Northwestern yet, but those are just minor technicalities. Since we're on the subject, I should also mention that I'm well aware Northwestern doesn't send out early acceptance letters until December 15, but, fearing that I may apply somewhere else, I'm sure they've made an exception for me. I'm positive my acceptance letter is on its way from the admissions office and will soon be in my eager hands as I write this…right?

I wouldn't be surprised if I was the first applicant. I stayed up half the night to submit my application as soon as the admissions website opened at 6 a.m. Chicago time on the first day. Now it's just a waiting game…and waiting has never been my forte.

I can't imagine why they wouldn't accept me. When they read my transcripts they'll see I'm a very liberal-minded young man in a very obstinate world begging to be rescued by means of education: a diamond in a pile of cow shit, if you will.

That and the fact that I'm one-sixteenth Native American and one-thirty-second African American (okay, that part I can't actually prove) should make me an admissions jackpot!

Even if that doesn't work, my high school career should speak for itself. I've kept my grade point average at an impressive 4.2 since freshman year. I've single-handedly edited the *Clover High Chronicle* since sopho-more year, and I've managed to keep the Writers' Club alive after school despite its apparent death wish.

Not bad for a kid in a town where the most common intellectual question is, *Will he actually eat the green eggs and ham?*

I'm kidding (sort of). Look, I don't mean to constantly harp on my hometown. I suppose Clover has some good qualities too...I just can't think of any off the top of my head.

Clover is a place where the pockets are small but the minds are even smaller. It's tiny and conservative, and most of the people are really set on living *and* dying here. Personally, I've never been able to hop on the bandwagon and have been publicly chastised because of it. Having aspirations to leave makes me the black sheep of the community.

I'm sorry; I just can't muster up pride for a town whose most cosmopolitan area is the Taco Bell parking lot on a Saturday night. And although I've never lived anywhere else, I'm pretty sure normal Sweet Sixteens don't consist of group cow-tipping.

When they built the first movie theater here, people lost their damn minds. I was only three, but I still remember people crying and cartwheeling in the streets. The line to see *You've Got Mail* circled the town.

I pray we never get an airport—who knows what kind of cult-sacrificial suicides might occur?

Yeah, I'm a little bitter because I'm one of *those* kids: bottom of the food chain, constantly teased, despised, an annoyance to everyone around them, most likely to find a pile of flaming manure on the roof of their car (oh yeah, it happened), but what prevents my life from being a sad after-school special is *I don't give a shiiiit.* I can't reiterate enough, this town is full of morons!

Whenever my pen pals from the online Northwestern chat rooms and forums ask me, "Where is Clover?" I'm usually forced to say, "It's where *The Grapes of Wrath* ended up." And that's putting it nicely.

Let's be honest: Go to the corner of Nothing and Nowhere, make a left, and you'll find Clover. It's one of those cities you pass along the side of a freeway, home to barely ten thousand citizens, that makes you ask yourself, "Who the fuck would live there?" Well, if you've recently asked yourself this in a car, the answer is, *This fucker.* Hi, I'm Carson Phillips, if I haven't introduced myself formally.

I read once that all great writers have issues with their hometowns; guess I'm no exception. You can't let your origins bring you down, though. You don't get to pick where you're from, but you always have control of where you're going. (That's a good quote; I'll have to remember to say that if I'm ever receiving an honorary doctorate one day.)

But this all just fuels my fire even more. Ever since I was eight years old and got asked, "What do you want to be when you grow up?" and replied, "The editor of the *New Yorker*," the looks I'd receive after the declaration—as if I had said "dragon slayer" or "transvestite golfer"—always pushed me a little closer to a metaphoric exit sign.

Perhaps that's why my issues with Clover started at such a young age. I was constantly shot down by nitwits who couldn't think outside the box—especially in elementary school, aka the first place they try to brainwash you in a small town.

I remember my first-grade teacher was giving a lesson on subtraction.

"When one thing takes another away, what do we call that?" she asked my class.

"Homicide!" I called out, so proud of myself. I wasn't technically *wrong*, but the look she gave me for the following three minutes made it appear that way.

The same year we had Founding Fathers' Day, and I remember it like it was yesterday. I walked to the front of the classroom, clutching the report I had spent hours on, and told the class everything I had learned.

"Most of the founding fathers were closeted homosexuals and slave owners," I said. Needless to say, I wasn't allowed to finish the report.

That day after school was the first day my parents were called in for a "meeting." It was the beginning of the complex relationship I have with the public education system.

"He's eccentric, so what?" my mom told the teacher.

"Mrs. Phillips, your six-year-old son told his class the presidents who founded this nation were homosexual slave owners," the teacher said. "I'd say that's more than eccentric behavior."

"That might have been my fault," my dad said. "He asked me for a funny fact about the founding fathers, so I gave him one."

"He was asking for a *fun fact*, you dipshit!"

Mom scolded him. "I told him to ask you! No wonder he's having trouble in school—his father is a moron!"

"Actually, Mrs. Phillips," the teacher said, "on the first day of school he introduced himself and told the class *you* had told him he was named Carson because Johnny Carson was on television while he was...*conceived*."

To this date, I've never seen my mother gulp so hard.

"Oh," she said. "Well, I take responsibility for that one."

That was the last time my parents were seen together in public. As you may have guessed, I'm one of those cynical kids from a broken home, too.

Until I was ten and saw a friend's parents interact, I never realized that people got married because they wanted to, because they *loved* each other. I had always thought it was more like jury duty: You got an envelope in the mail telling you when, where, and who you were required to reproduce with.

There was about as much love between Neal and Sheryl Phillips as there was between the squid and the whale. At least they had an ocean to share and not a three-bedroom, two-bathroom suburban home.

I'm pretty sure their wedding vows went something like this:

"Neal and Sheryl, do you take each other as your awfully selected spouse; to reprimand and scold from this day forward; for better but mostly worse, in counseling and in therapy, in anger and in frustration, to hate and then resent; from this day forward until death that you cause?"

Maybe at one point they loved each other, or thought they loved each other. But once you reach a certain age in Clover all that's left to do is get married and have kids. It may not have been the best idea, but it was what was expected of them, and they were victims of the pressure.

My mom was definitely in it for the long haul, always trying to make things work between them. Their marriage was a constant pattern: My dad was unhappy, my mom tried to fix it, my dad was still unhappy, my mom resented trying to fix it, there would be a massive argument, and the cycle would repeat.

Unfortunately my dad didn't want it to work; he had wanted out as soon as he got in.

At one point my mother quit her job as a receptionist at a doctor's office because my dad was, and I quote, "tired of picking Carson up from that fucking school." Not that his job as a real estate agent kept him working late; he just tried avoiding as much fatherly responsibility as a priest in a whorehouse. (I'm sorry, super proud of myself for that reference.)

Sometimes I swear I can still hear them yelling in the kitchen. Whether it was over a missing fifty bucks in their checking account or just a dish left in the sink, from nine to ten o'clock every night they were sure to be arguing. At least something was consistent in my childhood.

Our next-door neighbors used to watch from over the fence every night. I tried selling them popcorn one time but they didn't go for it.

Our *Titanic* of a family sank deeper and deeper as time went on. But in a sick way, I'm almost glad it did. In my desperate attempt to escape it, I was led to the greatest discovery ever: *words.* I was fascinated by them. There were so many! I could tell a story, I could write about my day, I could write about the day I wished I had had instead....It was an endless power!

Every time I would hear my parents going at it, I would open up my crayon box and notebook and go to town. Suddenly, everything became white noise and nothing bothered me anymore. It's how I held on to sanity in a crazy house.

Things with my parents came to a peak after Grandpa, Mom's dad, passed away. Grandma came to live with us a year later when she was diagnosed with Alzheimer's.

She had always been my champion and savior. Whenever I was having trouble in school she would sit me on her lap and say, "Don't let that teacher make you feel like you're anything less than brilliant, Carson. She's just pissed that the governor changed her pension plan."

It was hard to watch her slowly fade away. Even as a kid I knew something was wrong.

When she was at home she was usually in the linen

closet wondering how her room had gotten so small. Our neighbors used to find her wandering the streets alone, wondering where she had parked the car she didn't have anymore.

"This is the third time she's been found wandering around town," Dad said to Mom one night at nine o'clock.

"She just gets a little confused and forgets what the house looks like," Mom said. "What's your excuse?"

"I'm serious, Sheryl," Dad said. "Either she goes, or I go!"

It was the first time I'd ever seen Mom speechless. I helped her pack Grandma's things the next day.

Although she was getting more senile by the second, Grandma knew what was happening the day we put her in the Clover Assisted Living Home. She was very quiet and kept to herself. Mom did too, feeling the guilt of it all, I suspect.

"Why are you moving?" I asked Grandma.

"Because the people here are going to take good care of me," she said.

"Can't I take good care of you?" I said.

"I wish, honey," Grandma said, and stroked my hair.

I felt so helpless, but I tried cheering her up the best way I knew how.

"I wrote you a story, Grandma," I said, handing her a paper.

"Oh? Let's see," she said, and took it from me. "'Once upon a time, there was a boy.'" She stopped reading—not because she wanted to, that was just all I had written. "Well, it's a lovely story, but it could use some development." She smiled.

"Mom said I can visit you every day after school. She said I could ride my bike here," I told her. "I can bring you a new story every day!"

"I'd like that," she said, a little teary-eyed, and hugged me. She was sad but I was so happy I could give her *something* to look forward to. And to date, I've never missed a day.

Despite my mom's final attempts at making her marriage work, Dad eventually left when I was ten.

The whole neighborhood remembers that night. It was the series finale of *The Neal and Sheryl Show* and started at nine on the dot and stretched into the early hours of the morning.

"You can't leave now! We just started going back

to counseling!" Mom screamed after him as he went to his car. He didn't even pack, really; he just grabbed as many things as he could on the way to the door, including some Aztec decoration off the walls. Not sure what he was going to do with that.

"I can't spend another second in this house!" Dad yelled back at her.

He drove off, tires screeching, into the night. Mom ran after his car, screaming, "Go! You can't come back! I hate you! I hate you!"

She collapsed in the front yard and cried hysterically for another hour. It was the first time I realized just how much she cared about him. Thank God for the sprinklers; otherwise she might have been out there all night.

It's been me and Mom ever since. Well, there was that one time Grandma escaped the assisted-living home and wound up back with us for a day or two, but mostly it's been just the two of us.

Life without Dad was very different, mostly quieter. Even though Mom did try to pick her nine o'clock fights with me for the first couple of years, the house became pleasantly peaceful.

We found ways around having a grown man in the house. Mom never figured out how to put together the Christmas tree or lights, so she just told people in the neighborhood we converted to Judaism. There's no one here to fix things, so small things have been broken for years around the house (and I'm certainly not gonna take a screwdriver to anything).

Mom's never really recovered from the whole thing. She never went back to work, deciding to just live off the money Grandpa left us. She never dated or remarried, replacing my dad with wine instead. (And oh, what a love affair it's been!)

She mostly spends her life on the couch these days watching *Judge Judy* and *Ellen*. She showers weekly (if I'm lucky) and has become known in town as "that lady who grocery shops in her bathrobe and sunglasses." Perhaps you've experienced a sighting?

I've only seen my dad twice since he left; once on my twelfth birthday and more recently at Christmas two years ago. Yeah, he's a real winner. He makes Carmen Sandiego look super reliable.

"Where the hell have you been?" I said the last time I saw him, not able to hold it in.

"I moved up north to the Bay Area," he said calmly, like he was telling me what he'd had for lunch.

"Why?" I asked.

"To find myself," he said.

I tried my best not to laugh at him but a smile broke through. "Still searching?"

He never responded.

I've spent a lot of time being pissed at my parents over the years. I've never understood how someone like me could come from people like them. I guess ambition is a recessive gene.

But I suppose I should always keep in mind that, through it all, I've still had it much better than others… until those people's autobiographies outsell mine in the future. Then I'll be back to feeling sorry for myself. (Unpopular opinion: Your story is only sad until you start making money off of it. Then I no longer feel sorry for you.)

Let me put a lid on the violin playing in the background and reiterate my original point: Life has been shitty, but *I'm getting out of here*. I'm moving onward and upward and I've never been so excited.

Well, I think my life story is enough of an entry for one night. I was originally skeptical about this whole journaling thing, but now I see how therapeutic it can be. I seriously feel less stressed than when I started. I feel really calm and centered and— *Oh shit, it's midnight and I still have Algebra 2 homework! Gotta go!*

What a DAY and it's not even over yet. It started this morning when I woke up at the crack of ass, like I do every day.

Can I please just say that it has been scientifically proven that teenagers learn and test better when they go to school later in the day? Which I suppose would be taken into consideration if school wasn't really just a government-funded day care meant to keep kids occupied. (I don't know about you, but I'm most prone to committing crimes between the hours of 6 a.m. and 3 p.m.! Thumbs up!)

I eventually stirred to life after the fourth or fifth time hitting the snooze button. I stumbled into my bathroom and discovered I wouldn't be going to school alone; there was a huge zit on the side of my face. Acne: God's way of reminding you that, besides all your other flaws, you aren't perfect. Thanks for the heads-up, God, almost forgot.

I got dressed, went into the living room, and, no surprise, found my mom passed out on the couch.

Only my mother makes every morning look like the morning after a Guns N' Roses party when I know for a fact she was just watching *Beaches* on repeat last night.

I yanked open the drapes and let the light in. Every day I hope this will inspire her to get off the couch. Every day I also worry the sunlight will finally cause her to burst into flames.

"Mom, wake up!" I said, hitting her with a pillow. "You passed out again."

She jerked around under the blanket like a seal caught in a fishing net.

"Wh-wh-what?" she said, finally becoming conscious.

"Congratulations, you survived the night," I said. I like to greet her in the morning with supportive comments so she knows I care.

"If you were a decent person you'd just let me sleep!" she grunted.

"If I were a decent person I'd *put* you to sleep," I said.

"Oh my God, my head..." She sighed.

"You know, the morning isn't supposed to hurt."

I brought her a glass of water and some Advil. She needed it.

I looked around the coffee table—or should I say, the wine and prescription bottle graveyard it had become.

"Are you sure you're supposed to be drinking with all those prescriptions Dr. Dealer is giving you?" I asked her.

"It's *Dr. Wheeler*, and why don't you just leave that to the professionals?" she said, and took the Advil. "Those warning stickers are for amateurs."

Over the last few years Mom has formed this sick relationship with her doctor. It's sick because half the time I'm convinced she thinks they're actually in a relationship. She literally makes up illnesses so she can visit him and is convinced if she doesn't call him once a week he *worries* about her.

If I had a patient taking more pills than Judy Garland and Marilyn Monroe put together, I'd be worried too. But I'm not sure she means *worry* in the same sense.

"Go to school, get out of here," she said, burying her face in her pillow. "And if I'm asleep when you get back from school don't you dare put my hand in a bowl of water again!"

I gathered up all of my school stuff and headed out the door. "'Bye!" I shouted back at her. "Love you too!"

When my grandpa died he left me his 1973 Corvair convertible, which sounds really great on paper. In reality, he left me a lemon, and since the car is the most stress-inducing piece of machinery of all time and he died of a heart attack, I think it's safe to say he left me his cause of death.

It doesn't start unless the key is in the ignition, the left passenger window is open, and the radio is turned to a Spanish classics station. Don't ask how long it took me to figure out this combination. If it still doesn't start when those three things are in place, the slamming of the glove compartment and a good kick on the rear license plate usually does the trick.

I have a neighbor across the street who I'm convinced chooses this moment every day to retrieve his morning paper so he can watch the struggle. That jackass drives a Mercedes.

One good thing about Clover is that people are

rarely late. Every location is about a five-minute drive from another, and it only takes about an hour to walk from one end of town to the other. Unfortunately, this also means everyone gets to the student parking lot at the same time.

Woof. *The student parking lot.* With all due respect to our veterans, I have yet to hear a war story that sends shivers down my spine more than flashbacks of the student parking lot. It's a place where adolescents, most of whom haven't even lived a full decade of wiping their own asses, are given keys to huge pieces of machinery than can potentially kill many in a matter of seconds.

Absolutely no traffic laws apply in the student parking lot. It's every man for himself.

Signaling? Don't worry, I'm psychic and know where you're going. Speed limit? No need, the pedestrians should have heard you coming. Red zones? Don't worry, girl on the volleyball team, that means it's reserved just for you! Parking spots? Take yours and mine! Take several! Take as many as your Toyota Corolla needs!

And if this daily war zone wasn't enough, survivors

then make their way inside to an even more hazardous environment: high school, society's bright idea to put all the naïve, pubescent, aggressive youth into one environment to torment and emotionally scar each other for life. Way to go, society! Best idea ever.

When I stop to think about it, there aren't many differences between a public high school and a state penitentiary. It's paid for by taxpayers. No one wants to be there. It's overpopulated. You make alliances in the yard. Shanking is frowned upon.

At least in prison, you get out sooner for good behavior. Maybe if I could graduate earlier I would filter what I say more; I'm sure my peers don't like being called "cattle" as I walk past them in the hallways. But if the hoof fits, *get the hell out of my way—you walk slower than a turtle on crutches!*

Luckily for me, I made it out of the trenches alive today (I say "trenches" because if the smell in the hallways after lunch on burrito day isn't gas warfare, I don't know what is) and into homeroom safely. Tragically, homeroom is Algebra 2.

My algebra teacher, who coughs every twenty seconds for no reason and who I suspect plays with Barbies on the weekends, wrote an equation on the board:

$$x^2 = -19$$

$$x = \sqrt{-19}$$

$$\sqrt{19 \times -1} \quad = \sqrt{19} \times i \quad = i\sqrt{19}$$

"Whoa, whoa, whoa," I said, not able to stop myself. "What's the i?"

"The i is an imaginary number," he said, and coughed.

"There are *imaginary numbers* now?" I said in disbelief. "Are there *unicorns* in the next lesson?"

Don't get me wrong, I'm a great student. If I'm having trouble with a subject I stay after school and get the proper tutoring I need for it. Given that, I do believe I have the right to say, *What the hell is Algebra 2?*

I understand we have to compete with China and Japan, but we also have to compete with Iran, and you don't see us in classes learning to drill oil or make nuclear weapons. (Although I would take that class in a heartbeat!)

What grinds me the most is that we're sending kids out into the world who don't know how to balance a checkbook, don't know how to apply for a loan, don't even know how to properly fill out a job application, but because they know the quadratic formula we consider them prepared for the world?

With that said, I'll admit even I can see how looking at the equation $x - 3 = 19$ and knowing $x = 22$ can be useful. I'll even say knowing $x = 7$ and $y = 8$ in a problem like $9x - 6y = 15$ can be helpful. But seriously, do we all need to know how to simplify $(x - 3)(x - 3i)$??

And the joke is, no one can continue their education unless they do. A student living in California cannot get into a four-year college unless they pass Algebra 2 in high school. A future psychologist can't become a psychologist, a future lawyer can't become a lawyer, and I can't become a journalist unless each of us has a basic understanding of engineering.

Of course, engineers and scientists use this shit all the time, and I applaud them! But they don't take years of theater arts appreciation courses, because a scientist or an engineer doesn't need to know that *The*

Phantom of the Opera was the longest-running Broadway musical of all time. Get my point?

The board of education should sit down with universities and high schools alike and create *options* for students. Let us take *business classes* that substitute all the same credits as algebra. I guarantee a semester learning how to start a small business would benefit people much more than knowing:

$$ax^2 + bx + c = 0$$

$$x^2 + \frac{bx}{a} + \frac{c}{a} = 0$$

$$x^2 + \frac{bx}{a} + \frac{b^2}{4a^2} - \frac{b^2}{4a^2} + \frac{c}{a} = 0$$

$$\left(x + \frac{b}{2a}\right)^2 - \frac{b^2}{4a^2} + \frac{c}{a} = 0$$

$$\left(x + \frac{b}{2a}\right)^2 = \frac{b^2 - 4ac}{4a^2}$$

But perhaps my proposal makes *too much sense* for the board of education. (I know they're aware of it; all my letters have to be going to someone.) Then again, if they were actually interested in making the education system work, they'd probably have adjusted school hours when it was *scientifically proven students do better later in the day!* Sorry, that one still gets to me.

I feel sorry for the class of 2020. By that time, every student will most likely have to pass *differential calculus* just to graduate from high school. Good luck, kids!

Crap, Barbie-man has spotted me. I think he knows I'm not doing my homework; he coughed in my direction. I'll write more later. Until then, I'll keep mental tabs of other world solutions as they come to me.

10/3 continued

There I was in the trenches, minding my own business, walking from English to chemistry, when out of the corner of my eye I saw something pink emerge from the counseling center.

"Hey, you!" a prissy voice shouted. "Smart guy!"

It was probably a little cocky for me to instantly turn around, but let's be honest: Who else would they have been talking to? It was my counselor, Ms. Sharpton.

"Come see me in my office!" she said with a large, overly white smile.

"I've got English," I said.

"Don't worry, I'll write you a pass!"

I rolled my eyes and sighed; I was a tiger cub caught by a hawk.

How do I describe Ms. Sharpton? Imagine if Sarah Palin, Paris Hilton, and Princess Peach had a love child of sorts. Now add even more pink and a splash of bleach. Get where I'm going with this? The former 1989 Miss Clover decided to become a high school counselor only after she flunked beauty school.

There was a rumor she bought property in Nevada and tried becoming a Real Housewife of Las Vegas, but the show never got picked up.

I usually try avoiding her office as much as I can. That much pink is unhealthy.

She sat me down on a couch in a little area next to her desk that she called her "sitting room." She was in every framed picture displayed, alone or with a small rat-sized dog. And since some of the photos were taken three decades ago, either she has a thirty-year-old dog at home or she trades it in every so often for a new one.

"Welcome to Career Day here at the counseling center!" Ms. Sharpton said happily.

Oh, screw this. I seriously would have rather been having a colonoscopy.

"I'm sure you saw our flyer," she went on. "We're calling all you kiddos in today to talk about your future career options. You know, like what you want to do—"

"I know the exact career that I want," I interrupted.

"Okay!" She clapped. "What is it, munchkin? An astronaut?"

"I want to be the editor of the *New Yorker* and the

youngest freelance journalist to be published in the *New York Times*, the *Los Angeles Times*, the *Chicago Tribune*, and the *Boston Globe*."

"Well, you've had some time to think about this, huh?" Ms. Sharpton said. I don't think she knew what all those publications were. "Okay, what about college? I can help you decide what college to go to!" She reached for some pamphlets by her side.

"No, I've got to get into Northwestern," I said.

"All right," she said. "Where is that exactly?"

She wasn't kidding.

"Illinois," I said.

"Never heard of it," she said. "But why do you need to leave so badly? You know Clover has a community college right here in your own backyard—"

"Look," I said, feeling a migraine coming between my eyes (I'm allergic to stupidity). "I've put seventeen good years into this town. People spend less time in prison for murder sentences—"

"Is that true?" Ms. Sharpton asked, but I went on.

"I've been the editor of the school newspaper and president of the Writers' Club since sophomore year just to better my chances of getting into that school—"

"Wow, that's so smart."

"So I've already applied and meet all the requirements; I just haven't heard back from them yet. I'd appreciate it if you could find out why," I finished, not sure if she was qualified for the task.

"Okay, and that is something *I* would do? *I* would call them?" Ms. Sharpton said. She seemed nervous, like the phone might bite her if she tried to use it.

"Yes," I said. "I will do anything to get into that school. *Anything.*"

"Okay, I am on it!" She gave me a thumbs-up. "But since you're here, would you mind filling out one of these application forms for Clover Community College? With every application, I get a point toward a Clover College juice cup and I only need three more."

And that's when I got up and left. I was afraid my migraine would turn into a cerebral hemorrhage if I didn't.

I wish I could say the day got better—I also wish I could say I have amazing abs—but neither is true.

My final class of the day was journalism. It's the only class I feel that's preparing me for life—*my life* at least. I love journalism. I just hate the people in journalism class.

The journalism class is in charge of putting together the weekly school paper, the *Clover High Chronicle*. When I was a freshman, the students in the journalism class were considered gods. The seven seniors it consisted of and I were the people of the *know* and the *now*.

Students used to beg us to write or not write about their school activities. I had a cheerleader slip me a fifty once to leave out the fact that she forgot to wear underwear during a home football game.

Unfortunately, like a medieval plague, graduation swept through Clover High and I found myself the only one left in the class the following year. Even the journalism teacher, who used to take the most devoted naps during class, just stopped showing up one day. The school couldn't afford substitutes, so I was forced to take charge wholly. (Come to think of it, I'm not sure if this is even legal, but whatever.)

I tried recruiting new members but no one wanted to join. I even went to the special ed class but they just pointed and laughed at me. Teenagers don't want to write unless it's 140 characters or less these days.

The school ended up sticking people in the class who didn't have enough credits to graduate (which I'm half thankful for, half convinced they did out of spite). So the former Clover High hotshots have been replaced with the cast of *Freedom Writers*.

The *Clover High Chronicle* is made up of myself, assistant editor Malerie Baggs, movie reviewer Dwayne Michaels, weather reporter Vicki Jordan, and El Salvadoran foreign exchange student Emilio López.

We'll get to them in a second.

"Last week's edition of the *Clover High Chronicle* was yet another disappointment," I said at the start of class. "We did have new material for every section, but once again, it was all written by me. This has to stop."

I eyed them all with intense disapproval. Vicki yawned.

"This is the *Clover High Chronicle*, not the *Carson Phillips Chronicle*," I reminded them. "Hopefully, this week will be different." And with a clap I directed the room's attention to Dwayne. "Dwayne, do you have your review of *Manslaughter III* ready?"

Dwayne may be the most useless human being I've ever encountered. He usually wears beanies, even when it isn't cold, and probably just pisses liquid weed at this point.

"Yes!" he said.

"Yes?" I said, trying to hide my surprise.

"Oh wait . . . *no*."

"No?"

"I went but I passed out," he said. "You didn't tell me it was in 3-D."

"It wasn't," I said.

"*Whoooa*," he said quietly to himself.

I could barely stomach the situation. One day I swear an ulcer is gonna rip out of me like *Alien* and I'm going to name him Peer Incompetence.

"Vicki, do you have your weather report ready?" I asked.

She looked at me, clueless—correction, she took an iPod earbud out of her ear and then looked at me, clueless.

"What?" she asked.

"Your weather report?" I repeated.

She half-consciously gazed out the window for a

second. "It's cloudy," she said, and put the earbud back into her ear.

"Great," I said. "Thank you, Vicki." At least it was progress.

Vicki Jordan is one of those "goth" students. Sometime during the eighth grade she ditched everything she owned that made her look alive and became the walking undead. She dyed her hair, smeared on some black lipstick, and discovered SPF 110.

Personally, I don't buy "rebellious phases." I think they're just dramatic ways of saying, "I have no *real* problems, so I'm going to dress differently and hurt myself so people think I'm more complex than I really am." I'm sorry; you can kiss my ass with your "inner turmoil."

You want to be "left alone"? You don't want to be "understood"? Then stop dressing up every day like it's Halloween, you whiny little bitch. Get over yourself, get some Zoloft, and stop being a fucking eyesore to everyone around you.

Apparently I feel strongly about that topic. Anyway, moving on…

"Emilio, do you have a section you'd like to tackle

this week?" I asked. I might as well have been talking to a picket fence.

"I love America," he said in his thick El Salvadoran accent. I think that's the only English sentence they taught him before he was sent to the States. At least Emilio has a real excuse for disregarding me.

Language barrier or not, that guy gets around. I've lost count of how many American girls I've caught that El Salvadoran Frenching. He's traveled across many borders just to put his hands below other borders. I'll stop with the metaphors; you get it.

"That's great, Emilio, we'll create a special patriotic section just for you," I said, looking over my notes. "Now what about creative writing? Does anyone have any essays or short stories or—"

"I've written a short story for the *Chronicle*," Malerie said, raising her hand.

"Let's hear it!" I said.

Malerie nervously stood up and made eye contact with everyone before reading.

"This is written by Malerie," she made clear, and began. "'It was the best of times, it was the worst of times, it was the age of—'"

"Malerie," I cut her off.

"Yes?"

"You didn't write that."

She looked at me very confused, as if I was telling a child she didn't actually come from the stork.

"But it's in my handwriting," she said. "But if you don't believe me…" She didn't finish the thought and just sat back down.

If the Pillsbury Doughboy had a sister, I imagine Malerie would be her look-alike. She's short and round and a little…*different*. I wouldn't say she's *slow*, I'd just say other boats make it to the island before hers. She struggles a bit with concentration, metabolism, and plagiarism…but who's perfect?

Malerie has also carried an old camcorder around for as long as I've known her. She films *everything*. I used to find it intriguing when she first joined journalism class, sensing there might be the potential for a strong reporter in her, but now that I know creative writing is her passion it just worries me. What does she do with all that footage?

I eventually reached my favorite part of class: *my assignment.*

"As you may have guessed, I'll be tackling another *local issues* piece this week," I informed them. "My article last week, 'Small-Town Sex Scandal,' was a huge hit on the *Chronicle*'s Facebook page....It was about Mr. Armbrooster, the health teacher who was fired after using Gumby and Play-Doh to teach lessons about the female reproductive system."

Crickets. Statues in the Louvre would have been more interested. The bell rang and, like dogs at feeding time, everyone ran straight for the door.

"Don't forget there's a Writers' Club meeting after school if any of you changed your minds about joining!" I called out after them. "Or changed your personalities..."

I went to the board and erased *Clover High Chronicle, editor, Carson Phillips* and wrote, *Writers' Club, president, Carson Phillips*. There's something about doing this that gives me satisfaction every time. Even with all the bullshit I put up with, I still take pride that these clubs are still around.

I usually spend lunch replacing old "Join the Writers' Club" posters with new ones, as they're pretty much always the first targeted by vandals. I find it painfully ironic that those illiterate bastards tag *YOU SUCH COCK* on posters trying to attract writers.

The Clover High club system is intense. There's really nothing to do in this town, so students basically have no choice but to join after-school clubs for their own sanity.

THE CLUBS:

The Cheerleading Club: Also known as the Future Trophy Wives and Soccer Moms Club. The cheerleaders travel around campus in a vicious pack, emotionally scarring innocent bystanders they encounter. Warning: They do everything as a team, including menstruate.

The Athletes' Club: Jock central. They don't just play sports and measure each other's organs; they also practice character-building exercises like "Smell My Finger."

The Yearbook Club: Freshmen, sopho-mores, juniors, and seniors alike gather here and put together pictures and memorable quotes that totally rewrite history so the lies they tell their grandchildren will appear truthful.

The Drama Club: A place where boys can freely dress up and wear makeup and girls can spend years afterward wondering why those boys never loved them.

The BSU: The Black Student Union is for our one black student. He may be alone, but the school has convinced him it's important to represent his community. (And by having a BSU, the school gets a major tax credit! Score!)

The FBLA: Thinking about becoming a business owner or entrepreneur? Well, then don't join the Future Business Leaders of America; that's not what it's for! This is a place to fight over who has the best cell phone and whose daddy makes the most money.

The Clover High Choir: It's where all the most talented singers at Clover High go to sing backup for the choir teacher's tone-deaf daughter.

The Debate Team: If you're fortunate enough to have been born knowing every-thing, join the debate team and argue with kids just like you. You can't correct an opinion, but these kids sure as hell will try.

The Celibacy Club: A coven of very unat-tractive girls who find it easier to "stay pure" and "save themselves" than admit that no one wants to sleep with them.

The FFA: The Future Farmers of America. I don't have a joke for this one, this shit is real!

The Clover High Band: Do you like playing instruments? Then join band so you can play for an unappreciative choir singing backup for the choir teacher's tone-deaf daughter.

Detention: I'm not sure it's considered a club, but they have by far the most devoted members.

And of course:

The Writers' Club: A place students can express their thoughts and creativity through the power of words. But ask anyone else and they'll tell you it's worse than detention and we apparently "SUCH COCK."

I sat at a desk in the journalism classroom after school today for forty-five minutes staring at the door. I knew today would be the day; the day when someone finally saw one of my posters and would be compelled to join the Writers' Club.

The door handle started to move and I sat up in my seat. I felt like an astronaut finally discovering life on another planet. The door swung open.

"Hi, Malerie," I said, a little disappointed. In the three years I've run the club, Malerie has been the only other member. The club was even *her* second choice; she only joined when she got kicked out of the BSU.

"I wrote another short story for the *Chronicle*," she said. "And this one I think you're gonna like!"

"Great. Let's hear it," I said, bracing myself for whatever I was about to hear.

Malerie cleared her throat and began to read from her notebook. "'Call me Ishmael. Some years ago, never mind how precisely—'"

"Malerie," I cut her off. "Did you actually write this?"

"No," she said, and slumped—well, slumped more than usual. "I'm a complete disappointment."

"Don't be so hard on yourself," I told her. "Writing takes time. Using your own words would help too."

"But I can't think of any ideas myself. I have zero imagination. All God blessed me with was this flawless complexion and really good table tennis skills." She lowered her head and looked at me helplessly. "Carson, how do you do it?"

I opened my mouth to speak but nothing came out. The question had caught me off guard; no one had ever asked that before. What was my process exactly? Where did it all come from?

"Don't try to find the ideas, let the ideas find you," I said, unsure if I even knew what I was talking about. "It's one of the most amazing experiences, finding something to write about, or realizing something for the first time. It comes out of nowhere and just hits you.

Then it's all you can think about and it goes through your body and tries to escape and be expressed in any way possible....It's a lot like...like..."

"Lightning?" Malerie asked me.

"Yeah," I said. "Like lightning."

I let it sink in for both of us. Even *I* was surprised by my answer. It may have been the first time I've ever talked about writing in the Writers' Club. Usually our meetings are spent talking about schemes to recruit new members or looking up the species of insects Malerie finds on the school bus. I've always spent so much time trying to inspire others to write I had forgotten what inspired me.

"Don't worry, you'll find something to write about someday," I told Malerie, and she smiled at me.

Malerie has really grown on me over the years. Her wheels may not spin as fast as those of the average car, but at least she has a pulse. She may be the closest thing to a sidekick I'll ever have.

10/4

Do you ever find yourself in those *dear God in heaven how did I get here* situations? The kind that make you think *please kill me now death couldn't be any worse than this* type of thoughts? Me too.

Twice a week for an hour after school I have to suffer through a student council meeting. While the other members of the council have all been "elected" to their positions, being the editor of the school newspaper entitles me to join in on the discussions.

They've tried to get rid of me countless times, and even though I would rather be in the Gaza Strip with a target strapped to my back, I fight them every time. It's called "freedom of the press"; look it up. Besides, if I don't sit in on those meetings I never know what's going on, and I've got to write my expository editorials on *somebody*.

What's the nicest way I can describe the student council members? They're the kind of people who come from good families, have never had to deal with any major problems, and will most likely never have to *work* for anything in their lives. That's strike one against them. The fact that they're also ornery, uppity half-wits is strike two.

One of them stuck a tampon on my back last week after the meeting. I walked around after school for hours and no one told me it was there. I'm still not certain who did it.

The student council is led by student body president Claire Mathews. She's pretty, popular, petite, a proud cheerleader, and I suspect she also shits cupcakes.

Her parents are queen-bee-breeding machines. Every Clover High class since 2007 has had to deal with the wrath of a Mathews girl.

Claire is the youngest of five (and hopefully the last). There's a rumor she had a younger sister, but she wasn't born as perfect as the previous girls, so they axed her like a runt, à la *Charlotte's Web*. I started this rumor.

Also on the student council is vice president and yearbook editor Remy Baker. Not that I would ever admit to having an intellectual equal at school, but

Remy is probably the person closest to it. She's smart, ambitious, and driven (sound familiar?). The difference is, Remy drank the high school Kool-Aid. So naturally, we clash like two horny goats fighting over a mate.

She uses her power for evil. Sophomore year, Remy "forgot" to put me in the yearbook. How the hell does someone "forget" to put a student in the yearbook?! She was just mad because my History Day project beat hers.

Physically, Remy stopped growing around the fourth grade. I'm not saying she's a hobbit—I'm above name-calling. I'm just saying if someone was missing in Middle Earth she'd fit the description.

Justin Walker is the sports commissioner and also the head of the Athletes' Club. He's so dumb if you handed him a box of rocks he'd probably stick one in the ground and say he planted a mountain. His older brother Colin Walker, who graduated when we were freshmen, is now the football coach, and Justin sort of lives in his shadow...if he's not chasing it.

I should also mention that Claire and Justin are dating. Yup, the head cheerleader and the head jock are *together*! Don't freak out, I know it's shocking! Totally not cliché at all! I'm sure it's true love.

The other student council members are Scott Thomas, the performing arts commissioner and president of the Drama Club, and Nicholas Forbes, the Student Council treasurer and president of the FBLA.

Scott Thomas has hated me since I reviewed him in *Les Misérables*. I said his performance was "shallow and unrealistic," because it *was*. I'm sorry, low-budget production or not, Jean Valjean would not have highlights or sneak onstage to sing the backgrounds to "I Dreamed a Dream." It was crap and I didn't sugarcoat the truth, so he can suck it.

Nicholas Forbes is the oldest son of the richest man in Clover. His family owns pretty much everything in town: the strip malls, the farmland, and I think a few of the citizens. His parents gave him an Escalade at his sixteenth birthday party, and although I wasn't invited, I heard there were iPods in the gift bags.

I doubt their real last name is even Forbes. I think they had that legally changed to piss everyone off. We get it, you guys hemorrhage silver dollars.

Just to review, the student council consists of

Claire Mathews (queen-bee bitch), Remy Baker (yearbook twat), Justin Walker (shit-for-brains jock), Scott Thomas (dramatic prick), and Nicholas Forbes (rich mo'fo). There may be a test and/or murder trial later and I just want you to have the facts straight.

"I have some really great news!" Claire began today's meeting. "I'm happy to report there will be enough trucks and trailers for all the clubs to have floats at homecoming."

They all gave theatrical sighs of relief. I twirled my finger.

I have a special notebook for student council meetings. It mostly has illustrations of various torture and execution mechanisms I daydream about experiencing rather than listening to Claire's biweekly power trips. This week I've been working on a guillotine/boiling water/electric chair combo.

"As excited as we all are for homecoming, we need to choose a theme for the Sadie Hawkins dance—it'll be here sooner than we think," she informed us. "Any ideas?"

"Fun Under the Sun!" Remy pitched proudly.

"That screams skin cancer to me," I said.

"It would be fun," Remy said.

"It's an excuse to wear flip-flops and bikinis to school," I added.

They began shifting in their seats.

"What about One Night in Paris," Nicholas suggested. "My family and I went over the summer and it was beautiful!"

"Ab fab idea!" Scott chirped.

"That's great!" Remy said.

They all nodded in agreement.

"If we go all out it might run us over budget," Claire said. "Nicholas, do you think your dad can cover it?"

"He's never turned us down before!" Nicholas said with a sleazy smile.

I mentally vomited and then said, "One Night in Paris? Like the *sex tape*? Come on."

The shit-wads all slumped in their seats. But come on, seriously? One Night in Paris? Were they out of their minds?

"Okay, fine, let's go with something a little more generic like Under the Sea," Claire added to the possibilities. "It was the theme of my parents' school dance."

"Well, if you aren't going for *originality*," I commented.

"We aren't!" Remy said.

"Great," I said. "Everyone can bring their *crabs*."

The shit-wads all became incredibly irritated with me. I don't know why they always get so bent out of shape—they're lucky I insult their ideas before another school does.

"I hate you more than I hate the Holocaust!" Remy fired at me.

"Bite me, hobbit," I fired back. (Guess I'm not above name-calling.)

"We don't have to listen to him; he's just here because he's the editor of that stupid paper," Remy told the others.

"Dude, why do you care?" Justin asked me. "It's not like you go to them anyway."

"Because they're stupid!" I said.

"Fine, then you choose a theme, Carson!" Claire challenged me.

All the shit-wads turned and looked at me with menacing glares. Scott even snapped a formation in my direction.

"Okay," I said, and thought about it, but not too hard, as any idea I pulled out of my ass was going to be better than their asinine recommendations. "You all like TV, right? Why not do Famous Television Couples? People could be Fred and Wilma, Mulder and Scully, or Lucy and Ricky...."

They glanced at each other coyly. They knew my idea was the best, and it *sucked* for them.

"Heidi and Spencer!" Scott shouted excitedly.

"What?!" I said. "No...no, that's not what I meant—"

"Jon and Kate!" Remy said.

"Snooki and the Situation!" Justin said, and pulled up his shirt to show off his abs.

"Are you serious?!" I said. "That's reality television—that's ridiculous!"

But the damage was done. Tomorrow morning, they'll be announcing the theme for the 2012 Clover High Sadie Hawkins dance: Famous Reality TV Couples. And I am totally to blame for it.

Bastardizing my brilliant idea is strike three! I officially hate them.

I realize I hate student council meetings because they make me doubt myself: If I can't get *them* to listen to me, what makes me think someday I can get the world to? But then I convince myself that is a perfect example of how high school exists in a dimension of its own and does not reflect the real world.

I looked down at my notebook and added spikes to my execution/torture device before the meeting was over. It was soothing.

I spent quite a bit of time with Grandma after school today, more than I normally do. Usually I just sit with her for an hour or two and get my homework done while she talks nonsense to herself.

"And that's why I'm not voting for Nixon," she's declared a couple of times. "That man is so crooked he has to screw on his boots in the morning! Mark my words!"

But for whatever reason, today she said something that really struck something in me.

It started off like any daily visit. I drove to the Clover Assisted Living Home right after school; thankfully I made it out of the student parking lot alive. I waved at Kathy, the home's receptionist, as I walked past the front desk and down the hall to Grandma's room. (Kathy has never waved back. I've never even seen her blink. She just stares at the front door all day long. I'm thinking her title of "employee" may change to that of "patient" very soon.)

"Hi, Grandma," I said when I walked through the door. She was sitting on her bed, knitting a creation of some kind.

"Who are you?" she asked me with big eyes. Hearing this hurts every time.

"It's Carson," I always say back to her. "Your grandson."

"No," she said, shaking her head. "My grandson's just a little boy."

"I got bigger," I said with a shrug.

For a split second I could have sworn she recognized me, but I may have just been hopeful. She got out of her bed and headed out the door.

"I'll be right back," she said.

A few minutes passed and I sat down and started my homework. I could hear her talking to one of the nurses outside.

"I need to use the oven," she said.

"You can't use the oven," the nurse said.

"But I have a guest—he might be hungry," Grandma insisted.

A couple more minutes later Grandma returned with a paper plate full of Oreos.

"Here we are, fresh from the oven," she said, smiling, and handed me the plate.

I couldn't help but grin. "Thank you." I reached into my bag and handed her last week's *Chronicle*. "I brought you the latest edition of the *Clover High Chronicle*."

She took it and glanced down at it for only a second and then back at me.

"My article is called 'Small-Town Sex Scandal,'" I said. "It's just like 'Janitorial Genocide,' the other article you liked so much—"

"Do you know my grandson?" she asked me.

She's asked me this a million times, but I don't think you can ever get used to a family member asking you who you are.

"I think so," I said.

"I miss him," Grandma said, and her eyes became sad. "He never comes to visit me anymore. He used to write me stories." Her face began to light up again.

"Did he?" I asked.

"I remember the first story he ever wrote me," she said with a big smile. "'*Once upon a time, there was a boy.*'" She let out a long chuckle.

"I remember too," I said. As weird as this feels to say, I was really happy the memory had survived the crash.

"I told him it could use a little development, so the next day he brought me another story," she said. "*Once upon a time, there was a boy who wanted to fly.*"

I had completely forgotten about that.

"I'm worried about my grandson," Grandma said, and her face became sad again. "He's changed over the years. I think his parents are about to divorce, you see. He used to be so happy, but now he walks around with so much negative energy. Sometimes a personal rain cloud can be deadly, you know."

She walked to the window, nodding her head, and looked at the garden outside. Even with Alzheimer's, she still had poignant things to say. She looked back at me, about to add something else to her point, but I could tell it was lost when she made eye contact with me.

"Do you know my grandson?" she asked me again.

"I thought so," I said.

Grandma shrugged and went back to her knitting.

I finished my homework but stayed until it got dark;

I didn't want to leave her. It's a rarity to actually see *Grandma* when I visit Grandma, so I wanted to soak up the visit for all it was worth.

She eventually fell asleep and I decided it was time for me to go, but I thought about what she had said the entire way home. I know I'm bitter and a little jaded, and mildly enjoy it, but am I a sad person? Am I happy?

I plan on being happy in the future for sure, but it isn't here yet. So what does that make me, exactly? I've never been someone who could live in and analyze the present *moment*.

I got home at about a quarter to ten. There were fresh prescription bottles from the pharmacy on the kitchen counter, so I was happy to see Mom had made it outside, even if she was lured by drugs. She was sitting on the back patio, looking up at the stars, drunker than a skunk.

"Where have you been?" she said.

"Munich," I said.

She rolled her eyes. "Some people get to go home to wonderful fiancées and sonograms, and I get a smart-ass kid I never even wanted in the first place."

This may seem like an incredibly harsh thing

for her to say to me, but I'm used to my mother's drunken laments. I'm guessing she had seen someone pregnant at the pharmacy and it had sent her over the edge. Anything that reminds her of my dad is a sore subject.

"I was unwanted, huh?" I said.

"Never have a kid to save a marriage—it doesn't work," she went on. "I could have been something! I could have been a *pharmacist*! But I settled for settling down because I thought that's what I wanted, because that's what I thought *he* wanted."

"It's never too late to change your life, Mother," I said to her.

"It was too late years ago," she said—or slurred, rather. "You're lucky, Carson. You're young and naïve. All those dreams you have about getting out of this town and becoming something still seem reachable. You should hold on to that for as long as you can."

And after she said that, her eyes became watery.

"Good night, Mother," I said, and went back into the house. I was afraid if I listened to her grumble any more I might believe her.

I guess Grandma's not the only person in my life who talks nonsense. Luckily for me I've learned to only take to heart what the woman with Alzheimer's says.

Good night. Thank God it's Friday.

10/8

I hate Mondays with every fiber of my being. So granted, I was in a bit of a mood since this morning, but this day can go lobotomize itself. It started where I believe the core of all mankind's frustration begins. You guessed it! The student parking lot.

I was just about to pull into a parking spot (I even had my blinker on, which is pointless) when this huge Jeep came out of nowhere and stole it. If I hadn't slammed on my brakes at the exact moment I saw it, my car and I would be in pieces right now.

It was being driven by some stupid girl on the softball team. She wasn't paying attention to anything except the three friends she was giving a ride to school and the horrible music that was blasting from her speakers.

That's not even what bothered me. What really chapped my ass was her bumper sticker: IT'S A JEEP THING—YOU WOULDN'T UNDERSTAND.

For whatever reason, it just lit a fuse inside of me. I

got out of my car, slammed the door, and walked right up to her window.

"Hey!" I said, and banged on the glass. She looked me up and down, made some little noise in the back of her throat, and turned back to her friends. "I know you can hear me! Your car doesn't have a roof!"

"Can I help you?" she said through her nose.

"Yes, you can," I said. "I was wondering what it is that I don't get?"

"Whaaa?" she said. She was so stupid she couldn't even pronounce a proper *t* sound.

"Your bumper sticker," I said. "I don't get it. What exactly am I incapable of understanding because I don't drive like Crocodile Dundee?"

"Dude, you need to change your tampon," the Jeep girl said, and her friends cackled.

"I can't use a tampon if I'm dead," I shouted. (Yes, it was lame.) "Learn to drive!"

I got back in my car and found a spot across the lot.

So like I said, I woke up in a mood and the rest of the day didn't improve it. I battled through a typical day of incompetence and juvenile encounters. Some jackass fed Pepto-Bismol to the seagulls during lunch so there was bird shit and innards everywhere. Poor custodians.

Finally, I made it to journalism. I was hoping and praying something would happen there to better the day. I was hoping Dwayne had seen *Manslaughter III* again and remembered it this time. I was hoping Vicki would have at least written down *it's cloudy*. I was hoping Malerie would have at least changed a word in each sentence she copied.

My grandpa had a saying before he died: You can hope in one hand, shit in the other, and see which is filled first.

Hoping got me nowhere. Those fuckers didn't do a damn thing.

"We print tomorrow and none of you have written anything!" I said.

"I collated these kitten pictures," Malerie corrected me, and showed me a stack of cat pictures she had printed from the Internet. Not sure what the hell she was planning to do with those.

"Do any of you actually want to be here?" I asked them.

"*I* want to be here," Malerie said, and gestured to her cat pictures.

"Well, it looks like I'll be here all night, doing what you all should have done, again," I said.

"Will you cut the soliloquy short?!" Vicki blurted out. "This doesn't matter! No one reads the *Chronicle* anyway!"

"The art classes use it to papier-mâché things," Dwayne said.

I jerked my head in his direction. Was he telling the truth? He must have been; Dwayne is too brain-dead to be purposely snarky. Well, it got to me and I went silent. I hate looking vulnerable in front of them.

The bell rang and they scattered like roaches. Vicki stayed behind. I hated the way she was looking at me; pitying me. Nothing makes me feel more pathetic than when the *goth girl* feels sorry for me.

"Carson, why do you care so much?" she asked me. "Just don't...okay?"

She left with the others and I was alone in the journalism classroom. I took a beat to think about what she had said. I suppose to her it wouldn't make sense why

I'm always so passionate. But did it to me? Did running a failing high school newspaper really make my future more secure?

"Because I *need* something to care about," I admitted to myself. I think I hate showing vulnerability to myself more than I do to other people.

I considered just reprinting an edition from last month. Since no one "reads" the *Chronicle*, I supposed no one would notice. But had I done that, I would almost have been proving them right, and I'd rather shit broken glass bottles than let them win.

So I've been sitting here in the journalism classroom for the last four hours after school trying to pull another edition of the *Clover High Chronicle* out of my ass.

Speaking of which, I've had to pee for the last hour and a half. God, I hope the bathrooms are still open.

10/8 again

So…I've just been staring down at this journal for the last twenty minutes trying to find the words to describe what just happened in the boys' bathroom…. Then again, I'm still not sure what exactly just happened.

I walked down the hall (I don't call it a trench when everyone has gone home) to the bathroom. I'm usually the last one at school, so I was just happy it was open…and apparently so were others.

The sound of giggling (yes, giggling!) and moaning hit me as soon as I walked through the door. Oh yeah, people were getting it on in there! Is that not the grossest thing you've ever heard?

I looked down and saw two pairs of feet under a bathroom stall. I cleared my throat, letting the stall lovers know they had company. They totally weren't expecting it and panicked. I *thought* I could slightly recognize the little whispers through the quick rustling that happened after, but nothing could have prepared me for what was next.

Nicholas and Scott burst out of the stall pulling up their pants. NICHOLAS FORBES and SCOTT THOMAS!!! Take a minute to breathe—I needed to. Let's do it together, breathe in...hold it...and breathe out. You feel better? Me either.

Look, I guess in the back of my mind I knew it was only a matter of time before I caught Scott playing doctor in the bathroom with some little sophomore squeeze he met on Grindr, but the fact that it was with Prince Nicholas Forbes of Clover...Duuude, I can't even.

Thank God I didn't have any pencils on me. I wanted to gouge my eyes out.

"Gentlemen, I must say I am shocked. *Amused*, but shocked!" I said to them after my mind had time to adjust.

Nicholas turned so pale he was almost see-through. Scott just looked annoyed he had been interrupted.

"You're not going to tell anyone, are you?" Nicholas asked, looking at me with an expression that was half *we're friends, right?* and half *holy shit, I'm screwed.*

"Go ahead; tell the world. We don't care!" Scott said.

"Shut up, Scott!" Nicholas said, and then slyly grinned at me. "My parents can't find out about this. My dad is friends with *Michele Bachmann.* They'll send me to a camp that prays for fourteen hours a day."

"Listen, Cagney and Lacey," I said, and smiled cleverly to myself. "I know what it's like to be an outcast. I wouldn't wish the struggles of an *outed* outcast on anyone. So I'm not gonna tell."

"Fantastic," Scott said, almost disappointed I was sympathetic.

"Thank you," Nicholas said, and color started to return to his face.

I was insulted they thought I was the kind of person who was going to spread their secret around. I run a newspaper, not a tabloid. Therefore, I instantly came up with a much better way to use the situation to my advantage than public persecution.

"But," I said, and they became very still. "Since I'll be keeping my mouth shut about, you know, your abilities *not* to..." I mimed a blow job, although I think they knew what I was talking about. "Perhaps you could return the favor."

Scott looked at me with a tiny smile. I think

he thought I had something kinky in mind. (I should add it was a *you wish* kind of smile, which pissed me off.)

"How much money do you want?" Nicholas said, and retrieved his wallet.

"Oh, have some self-respect!" Scott said to him.

"I don't want you to shit a dime for me, Nicholas," I said, and then squinted. "But you know what the *Clover High Chronicle* could use? A finance section and a weekly update from the performing arts department."

They looked at each other and then back at me.

"You want us to write for your *hideodous* newspaper?" Scott said, and quietly laughed.

The face I unintentionally made was proof that I wasn't kidding.

"For how long?" Nicolas asked.

"Until we graduate and go our separate ways!" I said.

"I'd rather you just tell the whole school," Scott said, giving me a dirty look.

"Shut up, Scott!" Nicholas said.

"You're gonna talk to me like *that* just because *he's* here?!" Scott said.

"We'll do it!" Nicholas told me.

I clapped my hands together as though a great business deal had been made. "Gentlemen, sharpen your pencils!" I said.

So, as of next week, Nicholas Forbes and Scott Thomas will officially be a part of the *Clover High Chronicle* team! I'm still in shock. Talk about being in the right place at the right time! Thanks, God, and it's not even my birthday!

Look, I know making two gay kids do something against their will for fear of being exposed may seem a little cruel (wow, is that what I'm doing?), but it's not as malicious as it sounds. And let me make one thing clear: I am an equal-opportunity extortionist.

I don't care what you are—gay, straight, bisexual, black, white, purple, cat, dog, or pigeon: If you're a douchebag to me, I will be a douchebag to you. And these guys have had it coming for a while.

Honestly, they're so lucky it was me who walked in on them "*serpent whispering*"—otherwise it could have been *really* ugly for them. This town is not a good place for…well, all of *that*.

My hat is off to them, though. However they

managed to discover one another in the trenches of Clover High is a mystery to me. It's kind of inspiring in a way. It shows there's always someone/something out there for you if you keep your eyes open.

I'll admit the whole sex thing is one area of my life I haven't fully investigated. For one thing, I think sex is highly overrated. Like seriously, does it really need to be the underlying factor in every television show and movie plot ever made? Do characters/people not just do things for the experience anymore?

I got so sick of it I just stopped watching TV and movies altogether. Show me a film geared toward my generation about finding self-worth and achieving lifelong goals and I'll be so happy I may punch you in the face! Everything is about who's sleeping with who, erections and orifices, being straight or not being straight, blah, blah, blah....It gets tiring.

I thought I was gay for about a week once (I think everyone does at one point). But I think it was just the girls *around me* that I found repulsive. Like really, who am I supposed to hook up with in the backseat of my car? Remy? Malerie? Ms. Sharpton? (I have to stop listing; I'm making myself sick thinking about it.)

And do I really want to experience something like intercourse for the first time with someone in Clover? Whom I'll awkwardly be connected to for the rest of my life? Why would I want to put in all that work and stress when I can ultimately get the same results by myself?

Then again, I don't necessarily consider myself a virgin, probably because I have such a penetrating personality.

Do you want to know who I have a crush on? Rachel Maddow. I know I'm too young for her and she doesn't play for my team, but do you want to know why she's my pinup girl? Because *intelligence* is sexy. There's something about being with someone who's mentally conscious that turns me on.

Honestly, after watching my parents fight for the majority of my life, I'm not sure if I even believe in relationships at all. I like being independent in all aspects of my life....I take that back, now I sound like I'm asexual or a chronic masturbator. Maybe growing up with all of that fucked me up much more deeply than I thought.

Oh well, I'm sure I'll figure it out one day. I've

put all that on my life's back burner; I have bigger fish to fry this year. And now that I have Nicholas and Scott on the *Chronicle*, things are looking up! (No pun intended.)

Shit, I still have to pee. I'll hold it until I get home—definitely not using *that* bathroom ever again.

10/10

I talked my way out of detention today. It wasn't the first time and it won't be the last.

I was sitting in government class when my teacher asked, "Does anyone know which administration was referred to as Camelot?"

"Clinton?" asked Justin Walker, who sits next to me.

"Nope, that was *Came*-a-lot," I said, and laughed hysterically to myself.

Let me explain why I made a bad situation for myself. First off, no one else got the joke except my teacher. Second, he teaches government; therefore he has no sense of humor.

"See me after class, Mr. Phillips," he said.

So after he was done lecturing about the importance of the branch system and made half a dozen horrible jokes trying to validate his existence by connecting with the teenagers, I approached his desk.

"*Yeah?*" I said. My tone could have been nicer.

"Do you think that joke was appropriate, Mr. Phillips?" he asked me.

"No," I said. "It probably would have been better received in American history." Once again, no sense of humor.

"Mr. Phillips, how many times do I have to tell you outbursts like that are completely inappropriate..." He kept going. I just stopped listening.

"Look, you're the one who sat Justin Walker next to me," I said. "Since elementary school, teachers have pulled this crap on me and I've never complained. Everyone thinks if you mix the idiots with the bright students the intelligence will rub off, but instead, every day I can feel my own IQ points fall out of my head."

"So what are you saying?" he asked.

"I'm saying if the entire education system is gonna focus on the children who *should be left behind*, exceptions should be made for students like me too!" I explained. "And that's how I learn, with crass sarcasm."

"Mr. Phillips..." He sighed and rubbed his eyes. If this guy retires early I may be responsible for it.

"How was my joke worse than the one you made comparing the three branches of government to the

Three Stooges?" I asked. "At least my joke had valid historical facts to back it up."

"Just go, Carson," he said, and shooed me toward the door.

I figured my constant battle with the world would continue in English, but when I got there I found a note on my desk. It was written on a heart-shaped Post-it note and said:

Hey, smart guy, I heard back from Northwestern. Come see me in the counseling center when you can. Huggles, Ms. Sharpton.

Naturally, I ran straight there—I didn't even tell my English teacher I was leaving. I didn't think it was necessary; I'm willing to bet we weren't going to discuss anything about *Hamlet* that hasn't already been covered in the last four hundred years.

I burst into Ms. Sharpton's office. I felt l like I was finding out the results of a pregnancy test.

"You heard from Northwestern?!" I shouted.

Ms. Sharpton practically fell out of her seat. "You scared the crap out of me!" she said. She was having lunch and was consuming a sandwich twice the size of her body. She happily pointed to a huge green cup with a large *CCC* on it.

"I got the juice cup!" she told me excitedly. "It's limited edition, too!"

I didn't give a rat's ass and I think my face made it clear.

"Okay, yes, I heard back," she said. "That is a fancy-schmancy school you're looking at up there; they actually put me on hold when I called."

"And?" I said, begging her with my eyes to get to the point.

"Well, I didn't find out whether you've been accepted or denied," she said casually. "But the person I talked to said that high school newspapers and clubs aren't cutting it anymore."

Shit. "If you want to impress them, you'll have to submit something else," Ms. Sharpton said.

"Like what?" I asked.

"Um, I wrote it down...." she said, and gave me a dirty look, upset I was interrupting her lunch.

I gave her a look that said, *Bitch, this is my future we're talking about. Your sandwich can wait.*

"Okay, let's see," she said, flipping through a folder by her side. She found a tiny note she had scribbled it down on. "You could submit a novel, a book of poems....I can't read the rest of my handwriting."

"I'm not a novelist and I'm not a poet. I'm a *journalist*," I reminded her.

"I know, I know," she said in a mocking tone. "You're a *journalist*. Well, what about a literary magazine?"

"A literary magazine?" I asked.

"Yeah, apparently it's not as common as a high school newspaper. But a magazine filled with your work and the work of other students would show you can inspire other students to write while writing yourself," she said in a very chipper tone.

Fuuuuck, I thought. But, like a captain discovering he had been following the wrong North Star, I immediately set sail on a new route. If doing this would help my chances just one eighth of a percentage, I had no choice but to do it. And since the Northwestern Early Decision deadline is November 15 I'd have to do it fast.

"Okay, I'll do it," I said out loud. "But how?"

"I don't know how to start a literary magazine."

Ms. Sharpton shrugged, her mouth full of sandwich. "But get permission from the principal first, because he can be such an *asshole....*" She turned red, which didn't match all the pink. "Um, I didn't mean to say that...."

I ignored her. My head was already in full motion planning a new course of action.

"Okay," I said, and headed to the door. I had one last thing I wanted to say to Ms. Sharpton, but I was having trouble figuring out what it was. "*Thank you,*" I said when I remembered. It'd been a long time since I had used those words.

I ran as fast as I could to the front office.

"You need a hall pass!" said a freshman hall monitor.

"Fuck off," I said, and continued running.

How was I going to get permission from the principal? He's a tough man to pitch to.

Principal Gifford is the tallest man I've ever met—a former American Gladiator, in fact—and you can tell he deeply regrets becoming a high school principal.

When you look into his eyes you know he's constantly practicing the mental exercises he learned in anger management. It must be exhausting having a voice in your head tell you to "breathe in…breathe out…count to ten," all day long.

Things have been rocky between us ever since junior year, when I tried convincing him to make reading the *Chronicle* a requirement for all the students and faculty. It was a two-month-long conversation and I sent him 1,893 e-mails during that time. I lost, but I still stand by the suggestion.

I ran into his office, which consists of one desk and several dumbbells, but the only person there was Ms. Hastings, his secretary.

Ms. Hastings is very young and pretty, almost *too* pretty to be working as a high school secretary. I get a weird vibe from her; a vibe that tells me she witnessed her boyfriend kill someone in a big city and now she's hiding from him in a small town….Maybe it's just me.

"Where's Mr. Gifford?" I asked.

"You just missed him," Ms. Hastings said. "He has an appointment with his urologist."

Both our eyes widened.

"I mean, *dentist*," she said, and blushed.

"When is he supposed to be back?" I asked desperately.

"He'll be back tomorrow."

"This is an emergency. My future is on the line," I told her.

She looked at me, a little afraid. "Well, you might still catch him before he leaves. He could be in the parking lot—"

Before she could finish, I was out the door.

I raced to the faculty parking lot. At first I didn't see him anywhere and my heart dropped into my stomach. Then suddenly, up ahead, I saw movement. I had mistaken him for a tree.

"Principal Gifford!" I called out.

He stopped and glanced over his shoulder. He started walking faster to his car when he realized it was me.

"Principal Gifford! I have to talk to you!" I called out, and ran after him. "I know you can see me!"

"I'm tired. What is it, Mr. Phillips?" he said with a heavy sigh. "I already told you I can't make the English teachers pass out the *Chronicle* or any biased publications."

"I have absolutely no inquiries or requests about the *Chronicle*," I said, catching up with him. "I want to start a school literary magazine."

He started chuckling under his breath.

"Why are you laughing?" I asked.

"Tell you what," he said. "You can start your literary magazine. You can start a hunting magazine for all I care. But don't ask me for funding. The school is broke."

I hadn't even thought about that yet. I usually just raid the teachers' room when no one is looking for the extra paper needed to print the *Chronicle* for journalism, but this would require much more than that, especially if I wanted to make an impression with Northwestern. I may actually have to go to *Kinko's*.

I would also need some kind of advertising, some kind of press release to let the school know this was happening....

"Great," I said. "I'd also like to announce it at the assembly tomorrow." I thought that'd be a good start.

He began to shake his head.

"It'd take three seconds!" I said.

"Fine," Gifford grunted. "For my own amusement if nothing else."

"Cool. Thank you," I said, and bowed awkwardly. I'm really not good at this whole "being thankful" thing.

I was beyond excited to let the journalism team know.

"Good news, guys," I told them in class. "On top of the *Chronicle* and the Writers' Club, I'm also starting a school *literary magazine*! Awesome, right?"

The silence was deafening. They looked at me like I had just told them I had leprosy.

"Whoa," Dwayne said. "You really like embarrassment."

"And I thought *I* was a masochist," Vicki mumbled.

"America is most beautiful," Emilio declared.

"Thanks, I'm very excited," I said. "It'll give the other people in school a chance to showcase their literary work. So, if any of you have something non-journalistic to submit, you know where to find me."

"Can I submit my short stories about savage children living on an island without any adults?" Malerie asked enthusiastically.

"No, Malerie," I said. "Because that's *Lord of the Flies*."

She slumped in her seat, and my spirits slumped with her. That's the moment I realized I was drowning in denial. This was going to be difficult.

On my drive home, in between the thoughts of doubt, I brainstormed how I was going to ask my mother for the money to start the magazine (only a couple hundred bucks, nothing too serious). I considered hiding her pills and then selling them back to her, but our house is too small to hide anything. I decided asking the *genuine* way might be my only option.

When I got home I was taken aback by what I saw. Everything was *clean*. All the counters were wiped off, the carpets were vacuumed, and the pile of dirty dishes had disappeared from the sink.

To my even bigger surprise, *Mom* was cleaned up as well. She appeared to have showered and put on real clothes for a change.

Of course, she was wasted and half passed out on the couch, so I knew I was in the correct house, but she had put herself together before that.

"Mom, what happened in here?" I asked her. "Did the city health regulators finally come or something?"

"Your father was here," she said sadly. "We're officially divorced now. Apparently a couple of years ago I forgot to mail back the divorce papers. He brought me new ones to sign."

"What?!" I said, having difficultly processing the information.

"Stupid me, I thought he just wanted to see how we were," she said, but I wasn't paying attention to her. "What's your problem?" she asked.

"All this time I've complained about coming from a broken home, when in reality, I was just a part of a dysfunctional family," I said disappointedly.

"Don't worry," Mom said. "You're still a bastard."

I shrugged. I suppose she was right.

I can't believe it took a visit from my father to get my mother to act like a real human being. Clearly she's in a mood; I'll ask her for money after dinner.

10/10 after dinner

I may have just experienced the most abnormal dinner in the history of the Phillips house.

Normally dinner between Mom and me goes something like this: I make a joke about the food, Mom tells me I'm rude and becoming my father, I make a joke about her hygiene, Mom tells me she's doing the best with what life has given her, I ask her if life is the one hiding her shampoo, and then we do dishes.

Perfectly normal, right? Well, tonight's dinner didn't follow that format at all.

It started when Mom randomly exclaimed, "You need to be on antidepressants!"

I looked up at her cautiously from my corn. Even though I was the only other person in the room, I wasn't sure she was talking to me.

"No way. You're medicated enough for both of us," I told her.

"Aren't you depressed?" she asked me.

"Currently, while having this conversation? Yeah,"

I said. "Everyone gets depressed—it's an emotion. People turn to pills before they turn to their problems these days."

"Sometimes pills are the only solution," Mom said, trying to validate herself.

"You're depressing me right now. Are you saying if I take a pill you'll disappear?" I asked.

"That was uncalled for!" Mom sent a dirty look across the table.

"And so are most prescription drugs!" I said. "We're living in a medicated society. We start drugging kids with ADD, which they *all have*, and it doesn't stop until death."

"*You* were on ADD medication as a kid and you turned out somewhat decent."

"No, I wasn't." I knew she had to be mistaken; I have absolutely no memory of ever taking anything growing up, even vitamins.

"I hid it in your food."

I almost choked, hearing this confession. She was kidding, right?

"I thought I was just really calm and mature for my age," I said.

"Nope, you were drugged," Mom said nonchalantly. "When your father and I began our divorce you started asking so many questions we found it easier to roofie you than to answer you."

I almost choked again even though I didn't have any food in my mouth. It must have been true; Mom forgot how to joke after Dad left.

All those early years of judging my peers for playing tag on the playground, for digging up worms and eating them, for coloring outside the lines in coloring books—it was all medically induced, not because I was superior to them.

"Well, it isn't dinner unless some form of my childhood foundation is shattered," I said.

I figured at that point I really had nothing else to lose. What could possibly shake up dinner more than discovering you were drugged your entire childhood? So I asked for the money.

"I need money," I blurted out.

"I give you an allowance," Mom shot back at me quickly.

"I need more money, like three hundred dollars," I

said, and continued before she could interject. "I want to start a literary magazine at school and need money to print the first hundred copies or so."

"No," Mom said. She didn't even pause for a beat to consider.

"Oh, come on!" I said. "I know you're rolling in it. Grandpa died and left us everything."

"Wrong," Mom said, and made a game-show-like buzzing sound. "He left me everything and you his car."

"What about my college fund?" I asked.

"Key word *college!*" Mom said. She wasn't going to budge.

I really wanted to run outside at that moment and scream, *WHY IS EVERYTHING IN THE WORLD AGAINST ME?! I JUST WANT TO GO TO COLLEGE, I'M NOT TRYING TO GO TO THE FRIGGIN' MOON!* But I remained seated.

I must get my stubbornness from Mom. The only way to deal with people like us is to play a game of give-and-take; I had to negotiate with her.

"Okay," I said, my stomach tightening from what

I was about to propose. "If I start taking antidepressants, will you give me the money I need to start my literary magazine?"

She looked up at me, silently contemplating the offer.

"Deal," she said. "Now pass me the salt."

Has anyone else ever made a deal with their mother to take prescription drugs in exchange for cash? This was my first time. Although, rest assured, if *Nurse Ratched* thinks I'm actually going to be taking the happy pills, she's sadly mistaken.

I excused myself from dinner shortly after that. Call me crazy, but I lost my appetite after discovering the woman who prepared the meal in front of me used to drug my food

Good God! Why does my life have to be a Robert Ludlum novel?!

All right, let's see where I'm at with all of this literary magazine shit: Permission from the principal? *Check!* Funding for the project? *Check!* Peer participation? *Jesus Christ, how the hell am I going to manage that?*

10/11

The ASSembly was today. That's not a typo, I say "ASSembly" because it brings out the ASS in everyone who attends. Even the janitors act like baboons, and half of them have crippling arthritis.

It was held, like it always is, in the auditorium. It's really hard for me to generate school spirit in a room I know is used for Alcoholics Anonymous every Monday night and Senior Pilates on the weekends.

The student council sits onstage during the assemblies, like royalty overlooking their serfdom. I'm not hard to spot up there. Just look for the guy who's staring up at the ceiling with eyes the size of tennis balls and not moving whatsoever; that's me.

Coach Colin Walker was the first person to speak to the hopping pubescent crowd.

"When I look around this room I am reminded of when I was a captain of the Clover High football team," Colin said. "It was the first time Clover High had been the number one undefeated team in the county!"

The room went apeshit. I was too busy staring at

a ceiling panel with a peculiar stain on it. Was that an air-conditioning leak or rat piss?

"And now, as your coach, I'm proud to say I've kept that title for Clover!" Colin said, and got a standing ovation.

One student was in tears and shouted, "I love you, Coach Colin!"

Big frigging deal! There are only three high schools in the county and one of them is for young fugitives.

"Tomorrow night at our homecoming game, let's show Lincoln High what Clover is all about!" Colin said, and raised a fist high in the air. I was unaware he was in the Black Panthers. "Let's pull a John Wilkes Booth on Lincoln High!"

The eruption that followed was insanely loud. I'm surprised it didn't knock down all the rat-piss-stained ceiling panels. Coach Colin leaped off the stage, ran through the crowd giving high fives, and left the auditorium.

I don't mean to offend anyone by saying this, but while I was watching Coach Colin speak in front of the school, I couldn't help but be reminded of those old videos on the History Channel of Hitler encouraging the Nazis.

They're both politically placed brainwashers, they're both encouraging the destruction of a neighbor, and I hate both of their guts.

Speaking of things I hate, Remy was next at the podium. They had three phone books placed aside for her to stand on so she could reach the microphone.

"Hey, guys!" Remy squeaked into the mic. She actually got a generous round of applause. Maybe my announcement wouldn't be so bad after all. "So I have some good news and bad news. There was a little miscommunication with this year's Clover High yearbook."

I sat up in my seat. You know I live for this shit.

"It's going to be titled *The Glover High School Yearbook*, thanks to the bad handwriting of a freshman girl whose name I won't say but rhymes with *Dally Desterfield*, so you have her to thank," Remy said. She made evil eyes at Sally Chesterfield, who shivered in the front row.

The last time I saw Sally she weighed an easy two hundred pounds, but the petrified girl I was looking at now couldn't have been more than ninety. It must have been a rough week.

"But the good news is, I was able to knock off ten dollars from the price!" Remy happily announced. "So they'll be sixty dollars each, not seventy. All preorders are still final."

She was done, and it was my turn. I had one shot at inspiring the people of my school to submit to my literary magazine. One chance to further cement my future...

"Hello, future farmers and inmates!" I said into the mic. "I'm Carson Phillips from the *Clover High Chronicle*, and I'm here with some very exciting news! This year for the first time ever, Clover High will release its first *literary magazine*!"

I clapped after the announcement. I was alone.

"Now, I know most of you can't read, let alone write," I continued. "But for all the secret writers out there, please submit any original work into the box outside the journalism classroom and it will be published. Poems, essays, short stories...hit lists, anything!"

I felt like George W. Bush campaigning at a San

Francisco town hall. It was awkward—really awkward.

"Thank you," I added to the ever-still crowd. "God bless."

Okay…so a couple of things I learned today after speaking at the assembly: Number one, know your audience. Number two, if you open with a joke, make sure not to offend everyone in the room with that joke. Number three, *DON'T SPEAK AT AN ASSEMBLY. WHAT THE HELL WAS I THINKING?!?!?*

I was completely desolate until after school, when I went to collect the submission box from outside. It was heavy and full! Maybe I had inspired people at the assembly after all.

I brought it into the journalism classroom. Malerie was there helping me build our float for homecoming—which is gonna be great. I can't wait to see it finished!

"I'm so excited for homecoming!" Malerie said. "Our float is going to be flawless."

"Yeah, the crowd is gonna love it!" I said, and opened the submission box.

The room instantly filled with a grotesque odor. A

family of flies flew out of the box and circled the room. The submission box had been used as a hazardous-waste basket.

Candy wrappers, tissues, used gum, half-eaten hamburgers, and the remains of what looked like a back-alley abortion filled the box, but there wasn't a literary submission in sight.

"Oh, no!" Malerie said. "*Shiterary* magazine." She pointed to the side of the box where some asshole had gotten creative with a Sharpie.

"Typical," I said, and sat down next to her. "I can't even run a school newspaper. I don't know why I thought I could start a literary magazine."

I felt a rush of defeat surge through my body. The big bright neon Northwestern sign in my brain went dark. I felt like it was over, there was nothing else I could do; I just had to sit and wait and hope for an acceptance letter the *traditional way*. It was the worst feeling ever—I felt like *everyone else*.

"Don't be too hard on yourself," Malerie said. "If you can get Nicholas Forbes and Scott Thomas to join the *Chronicle*, you can do anything."

"I'm blackmailing them," I admitted. "I caught

them playing Lewis and Clark in the boys' bathroom. Don't ask."

I know I had promised them I wouldn't say anything, but it was Malerie. I knew their secret would be safe with a girl who still believes in Santa.

"Oh," Malerie said. It took her a moment to realize what I meant by Lewis and Clark. "There seems to be a lot of that going around. I caught Coach Walker and Claire Mathews bonking each other in the boys' locker room."

I sat straight up like a startled meerkat.

"I just go in there to think sometimes," Malerie said, and blushed.

"What?! I thought she was dating *Justin* Walker," I said.

"That must be awkward," Malerie said.

I immediately had a mental image of dinner at the Walkers' house. Claire was sitting in between Colin and Justin. Both put a hand on her thigh and slowly made their way up her leg and finally *met in the middle*. (This image has been in my head all day like a bad Ke$ha song!)

To make matters worse, Malerie showed me the

actual footage of what she had seen. When I said Malerie films everything, I meant it.

What could have ultimately been the hottest sex video ever, a perfect cheerleader meeting the football coach in his office after school, ended up being one of the saddest things I've ever seen: Claire lying under Colin, checking her manicure behind his back while he thrust like a dog with arthritis.

It was enough to make you cry blood, and validated all my views on sex in high school.

"Too bad *they* aren't writers," Malerie said. "If they were in the literary magazine, everyone would want to be in the literary magazine. It would sell out for sure."

I looked at her closely. Was she implying what I thought she was implying?

"Just makes you think, though," Malerie went on. "Everybody has something to hide, even Claire Mathews."

She was!

"Yeah, I suppose you're right," I said. Had I not been so bummed about the whole assembly situation, I might have thought further into it, but the urge to gouge out my eyes after seeing that video filled up all my headspace.

Malerie and I finished painting all the pieces for our float. I think it's going to turn out really nice when we put it all together. Hopefully, by the grace of God, someone will see it tomorrow night and be inspired to join the Writers' Club. And maybe, just maybe, they'll be inspired to submit to the literary magazine as well.

It's three o'clock in the morning and I can't sleep. I've never been so furious in my entire life. I can barely move, I'm just lying in my bed *thinking…and reliving… and plotting.*

After the events at homecoming tonight I'm not sure I'm even human anymore. I'm just a creature made entirely from rage and humiliation. I was so mortified I thought my telekinesis was going come out and kill them all. I would smile at the thought, but I've forgotten how to smile.

Unfortunately for me and fortunately for all of those bastards, my telekinesis stayed inside. Sissy Spacek's gymnasium of death in *Carrie* and Jean Grey's carousel of cremation in *X-Men 3* would have looked like a basket of puppies compared to what I might have done.

Everything seemed so normal. School was fine. The trenches weren't too smelly. I actually understood a lesson in Algebra 2. I was in a *good mood*! I should have known then that the day was going to end in disaster.

I met Malerie on the football field after school to put our float together. Bit by bit we assembled our masterpiece. We made a giant notebook that actually opened and closed that said *The Writers' Club*, and on the inside said *It's the Write Club for You!*

We even had costumes to add a theatrical element. I was dressed as a giant number two pencil, and Malerie was a giant notepad.

"I'm having second thoughts about this outfit," Malerie said. "These horizontal lines aren't very flattering."

"You look fine, Malerie," I said. I didn't spend two hours creating an authentic notepad for her to get cold feet *now* (two pieces of cardboard and a Slinky, if you're looking for Halloween ideas).

We took a step back and admired our float once the final touch had been added. Sure, we didn't have the budget for a rolling Roman Colosseum like the cheerleaders had, or the means to rent a Corvette like the yearbook douches did, but we were proud of ourselves nonetheless.

I had tried selling ad space to local businesses but didn't have any takers.

Claire Mathews strode up to our float wearing

stilettos and a pink gown. She was nominated for homecoming queen and was expected to win—after all, she was in charge of counting the votes.

"You look like shit," I said. An insult coming from a life-sized school supply didn't faze her much.

"Why couldn't I have worn something like that?" Malerie asked me.

"I don't know what you're wearing, but I have some bad news," Claire said. "The truck pulling the cheerleaders' float, its engine just broke down, so we're taking yours."

She smiled, nodded, and tried walking away.

"Excuse me?!" I said, feeling actual steam emitting from my ears.

"I'm sorry," Claire said, looking back at me, "but homecoming is nothing without the cheerleading float."

"Go take the athletes' truck away," I demanded. "They pride themselves on running around like mules anyway!"

"I'm sorry, my decision is final," Claire said with a smile so fake my left eye started to twitch. She strutted off like she was on a runway.

My insides started boiling. I felt like I was being

cooked from the inside out and my anger was the chef. She couldn't do this to me—this was my last shot at making the literary magazine. I started pacing, trying to come up with my next move.

"Too bad," Malerie said. "At least we had fun making it."

"No," I said, and stopped dead in my tracks. "They're gonna see this float if it kills me."

I stormed off toward the other floats. I found a rope the cheerleaders had tossed aside. Suddenly, a lightbulb appeared over my head like a bad motel vacancy sign. I had an idea!

I bet you thought I went on a strangling rampage after that. That was my first idea too, but no, I pursued the second idea instead. I went back and tied the rope to the front of our float.

It could work....It just might work, I thought to myself. From that moment on, my body was running on pure adrenaline. I felt like the Hulk. (The Mark Ruffalo Hulk, not those other guys.)

Night fell...the game started...fireworks burst in the sky (which I'm assuming meant we were winning or had entered some kind of war)...the band warmed up the crowd with cheesy melodies from the seventies…and homecoming began.

There are moments in life when you think, *Oh my God, is this really happening? Am I actually doing this? Is this how I'm going to be remembered for the rest of my life?* This was one of those moments, and unfortunately for me, it was very real, I actually did it, and it'll probably be how I'm remembered for the rest of my life.

Picture me, dressed as a fucking pencil, *pulling* the Writers' Club float across the football field by myself. Imagine Malerie, dressed as a giant notepad, operating the giant notebook on top of our float and waving to the crowd. Visualize the crowd roaring uncontrollably at the cheerleaders passing by but then going dead silent once they noticed us.

It was so quiet all you could hear were my grunts and swearing while I was pulling the float.

"Yeah! Writers' Club! Woo-hoo!" Malerie enthusiastically shouted and continued waving.

A quiet rumble of snickering started, which grew into an eruption of giggling, which then evolved into an explosion of laughter. Everyone—the parents, the students, the faculty, etc.—was pointing and laughing hysterically at me.

"*SCREW YOU!*" I screamed at them, and finished pulling the float off the field. I was sweating profusely, my face was as red as Mars, my hands were bleeding from the rope, and my body had become so stiff I could barely walk.

I ripped off my pencil costume, got in my car, and bolted out of the student parking lot. *I didn't even use my blinker.*

I must have driven a hundred miles an hour all the way home. That sounds really fast, but the speedometer is broken, so I was really only doing like sixty or seventy.

I got home, went into my bedroom, and collapsed on my bed. The snide remarks from my peers, the discouraging comments from everyone else, and my own thoughts of doubt were on constant replay in my mind.

"*I'm sorry, but homecoming is nothing without the cheerleading float!*"

"*No one reads the* Chronicle *anyway.*"

"*The art classes use it to papier-mâché things.*"

I thought of the student council....I thought of the *Chronicle*....I thought of Ms. Sharpton and Mom....I thought of Grandma and Malerie....

"You're young and naïve. All those dreams...still seem reachable."

"The i is an imaginary number."

There was no way I could make the literary magazine work now. I had done everything I possibly could. *Except one thing...There was one thing I hadn't tried yet....*

"If you can get Nicholas Forbes and Scott Thomas to join the Chronicle, you can do anything."

"Nixon is so crooked he has to screw his boots on in the morning!"

"Everyone has something to hide!"

Before I could even think the idea through, I grabbed my cell phone and called Malerie.

"Malerie, it's Carson," I said. "Operation *Clovergate* is in effect."

It was decided before I even picked up the phone. I'm done being patient. I'm done being nice. I'm done letting them walk all over me.

Come Monday morning, I will get my literary submissions, even if I have to blackmail the entire school.

CLOVERGATE, DAY ONE.

I dismissed myself early from chemistry so Malerie and I could get started. I walked across the campus and found her in her art class. They were sculpting and Malerie was making a Bugs Bunny bust of sorts.

"Malerie, let's go!" I said to her from the doorway. "Clovergate time!"

"But I'm sculpting," Malerie said, looking around for her art teacher. The man used to teach wood shop; he wears an eye patch and is missing four fingers. Malerie ditching class was the least of his worries.

"Malerie, this is no time for sculpting!" I said. She looked like a confused puppy at a crossroads. She gathered her things with her elbows since her hands were covered in clay.

"Hey, it's that pencil guy from homecoming!" some jackass in the class said. I acquainted him with my middle finger and we left.

In the journalism room, Malerie and I made a large CLOVERGATE board. We put up the school pictures of who my first victims would be: Claire Mathews, Coach Walker, Remy Baker, Nicholas Forbes, Scott Thomas. My sights were set very high.

"Capture the queen, and the colony will follow," I said.

"Yeah," Malerie said. "Unless the ants revolt and execute the queen first like they did in my ant farm."

We added Vicki Jordan and Dwayne Michaels to the board. Like I said before, I'm an equal-opportunity extortionist; I wasn't only targeting the popular kids. Besides, I thought they'd make good diversity for the magazine.

"How are we going to blackmail all of them?" Malerie asked.

"I've got dirt on most of them," I said. "But I'm not sure about the others. Then again, Columbus wasn't sure North America was there. And you know what he did when he got here?"

"What?" Malerie asked.

"He enslaved every Indian around him," I said.

"Oh," Malerie said, and gazed up at the board. "All you little Indians watch out."

"Some will be much easier than others," I said,

deciding where to strike first. "Remember, Malerie, if anything happens to me while I'm attempting this, you're in charge of the *Chronicle* and the Writers' Club."

Her jaw fell open and her eyes widened. I had to tell her I was partially kidding and my life wasn't really at stake.

"Who are we starting with?" Malerie asked.

I walked closer to the board and examined Remy's cheesy class-photo smile. "I'm starting with Frodo," I said. "She's in my English class next period."

A few weeks ago, I stumbled upon a funny user name on the Clover High School website: Yearbook-Girl69. I didn't think much of it, a freshman slut under Remy's rule perhaps. However, whoever it was left uptight opinionated comments on almost every page.

"Why do the lunch ladies need to be at back-to-school night? Can't they just stay in the kitchen?" was one of the many obnoxious posts. "I hate lunch ladies more than I hate war!"

Could Remy be pulling a Voltaire? Over the weekend, while I was thinking of ways to blackmail Remy, I messaged YearbookGirl69 privately to test out this theory under the user name BadBoy2012.

"Hey, sexy," I messaged. "Love reading your thoughts on the CHS site. We think alike."

A few minutes later, she responded. "OMG thanks. I'm so glad some1 noticed LOL."

I waited a couple of minutes more, playing hard-to-get, seeing if she'd write more.

"Who is this LOL?" YearbookGirl69 asked.

"I like to keep my identity a secret; I'm like Batman," I replied. "But with better abs."

"Hott! Me 2! I like the mystery LOL," she sent. I don't know what the hell was so funny. Was she seriously laughing out loud every time? "Can I get a pic of those abs?" she asked.

I copied and pasted a picture of Taylor Lautner's torso from the Internet (I pray no one ever finds that Google image search in my web history).

"@Q#$TWERYJ#$%&!!!" is what I got next. "Are U even real?"

"Very," I said, and left it at that.

Now, today, while I was in English and the class had their laptops out, I decided to see if I was right about Remy. I was sitting a few seats behind her and had a clear view of her computer.

BadBoy2012 messaged YearbookGirl69. A window popped up on Remy's computer screen. *Bingo!*

"What are you wearing?" BadBoy2012 asked.

I saw Remy's neck blush.

"Practically nothing," Remy responded as Yearbook-Girl69.

"Send me a pic!" BadBoy2012 said.

Remy looked around the classroom to see if anyone was watching her. I ducked behind my laptop when she glanced my way. I looked back and saw her retrieving a photo from her documents and attach it to the instant-message conversation.

A photo of Remy half-naked with a "sexy face" popped up on my computer screen. It was enough to turn a nun into an atheist. I shut my laptop, ran out of the classroom, and vomited into the nearest trash can. I'm being dramatic—I didn't vomit but I did dry-heave.

"Mr. Phillips, are you all right?" my English teacher asked when I returned to class.

"I'm afraid I'm changed for life," I said, and went back to my seat. Remy rolled her eyes at me as I passed her. *She had no idea what she had just done to herself!*

After school I found Remy sitting on a bench alone.

I sat down next to her. I couldn't make eye contact. I'm not sure I ever will again.

"Can I help you, Carson?" she asked rudely.

I slyly handed her a large manila envelope. Inside she found printed copies of the conversations between BadBoy2012 and YearbookGirl69.

She went silent for a good minute and a half. Out of the corner of my eye I saw the papers start to shake in her tight, petrified grip. She looked at me as if I had told her that her father had had a successful sex change while she was at school.

"You're BadBoy2012?" she whimpered.

"I can't even look at you anymore," I said. "Not that it was easy before."

I took a bright yellow flyer out of my back pocket and handed it to her. I left before she could open it. The flyer said:

YOU ARE CORDIALLY INVITED TO ATTEND A
MANDATORY MEETING IN THE JOURNALISM
CLASSROOM FRIDAY AFTER SCHOOL.

I had to make sure it was subtle in case any of my victims tried turning me in, but if Remy's horror was any indication, *that* wouldn't be a problem.

I stopped by the boys' bathroom, figuring I could kill two birds with one stone. Unsurprisingly, I saw Nicholas and Scott come out of it at roughly the same time. They must have had a quickie.

"Hey, Siegfried," I said to Nicholas, and handed him a yellow flyer. "And here you go, Roy," I said to Scott, giving him one too. "Enjoy." I figure I pretty much have them under my thumb until I move to Illinois, so I didn't bother explaining things further.

I went to the journalism classroom and drew an X on Scott's and Nicholas's faces. I drew several X's on Remy's, just because I was still having trouble looking at her.

I drove home with a big smile. Three down, four to go! Clovergate Day One has been a success!

CLOVERGATE DAY TWO

I woke up this morning (which is always a good thing) and decided to hit the easy targets of my Clovergate plan. Yesterday's blackmailing worked out so well I didn't want to get ahead of myself. So today, I set my sights on Vicki and Dwayne.

It was lunchtime and all the high school beasts were roaming around the quad. I met Malerie in the shadows behind the cafeteria Dumpster. No one could know what we were up to.

"Did you get the stuff?" I asked her.

"Yeah," Malerie said. "And it wasn't easy." She pulled out a tiny Ziploc bag containing...*stuff.*

"Great work!" I said. "Let's find him."

Dwayne was sitting at one of the shaded tables in the quad. If the quad was a neighborhood, the shaded benches would be considered the "other side of the tracks." This is where all the slackers go at lunch to compare skateboarding injuries and bomb-building techniques.

Malerie looked around with large, worried eyes.

"It's okay, Mal," I said. "Just follow my lead. Good cop/bad cop, remember?"

"Yeah," she said, and toughly pursed her lips. "Let's do this."

We approached Dwayne and leaned in toward him from the other side of the table; the interrogation was on.

He looked up at us from a sketch he was drawing of a squirrel armed with grenade nuts. (I thought it was clever, but this was no time for praising the enemy.)

I tossed the small bag onto the table.

"What is that?" Dwayne said, tapping it with his pen.

Malerie busted out laughing and then immediately dropped into a serious gaze. "Come on, *you know what that is!*"

Apparently Malerie was the bad cop.

"You left this in the journalism classroom," I said.

He stared at us blankly. I wasn't sure if he was confused or just normal Dwayne.

"Did you guys want some?" he asked us, and a smile appeared on his stupid face.

Malerie looked at me; we hadn't planned for this response. I nodded to her: *Stay the course.*

"If we were responsible students, we would go to the school authorities," she said, violently pointing behind her. She was pointing at the janitor's closet, but Dwayne got the gist of things.

"Whoa-whoa-whoa!" Dwayne said, and his face changed more than I've ever seen it move. "Listen, I'll write that movie review you want, all right?!"

"It's too late for that," I said sinisterly, and slammed a flyer on the table.

I grabbed the Ziploc bag and walked away. I figured actions spoke louder than words. Malerie stayed there and continued pointing at him. I had to go back and collect her.

"Great job, Malerie!" I said once we were back in the journalism classroom.

"*I don't want to hear it!*" Malerie yelled at me and I jumped. She was still so aggressive. "Sorry, it's hard for me to get out of character."

"No worries," I said. "By the way, what was in the bag?"

"Crushed-up Funyuns, pencil shavings, and string," she said.

"Is that what weed looks like?" I asked.

"Weed? I thought you said 'tweed,'" Malerie said, and then looked down at the floor, as if the solution to her confusion was on the ground.

"Doesn't matter, he bought it," I said, and Malerie smiled again.

I went to the Clovergate board and drew a large *X* on Dwayne's photo. Vicki's was next to it.

"What do you have planned for Vicki?" Malerie asked.

I really had to think about this one. Vicki would be a tricky person to blackmail; she was so openly flawed. What does the girl with all the upside-down crosses and "Satanfest 2011" pins on her backpack not want everyone at school knowing about?

Then it came to me: Vicki might not be keeping anything from her peers, but what about her *parents*! Unless she was the love child of Ozzy Osbourne and Lily Munster, they couldn't approve of their daughter's behavior!

"Do you know what Vicki's parents' names are?" I asked Malerie.

"I do!" Malerie said. "Martha and Jebediah Jordan. I used to be in her mom's Sunday school class until my family converted to Lazyism and stayed home on Sundays."

I practically did a frigging cartwheel right then and there. "*Perfect!*" I yelled.

I immediately hopped behind my computer and Googled "Satanfest 2011." I never actually thought the pin had any meaning, like the Celibacy Club's purity rings, but boy was I wrong . . . and what I saw made me wish I had been right.

It was an annual gathering held at the fairgrounds convention center that attracted all the seriously fucked-up people from the local counties. Judging from the photos, it looked like the participants listened to heavy metal, pierced things, bought various wardrobe accessories made of chains, compared eye makeup, and drank the tears of innocent children. (That last one is purely conjecture—I have no proof.)

Unfortunately, the pictures got worse and worse. At one point I saw something like a goat under a tablecloth surrounded by a circle of candles. Fortunately, our Vicki seemed to be the muse of the photographer. Unfortunately, I saw more of Vicki than I wanted to, that's for sure.

I hit the print button on my keyboard multiple times and the erase-memory button on my brain.

"Now that I think about it, I don't think *Lazyism* is a real religion," Malerie said to herself. "I think my parents just hated church." She nodded very seriously and convincingly to herself.

"I think you're right," I said, and nodded along. I collected the pictures from the printer and went on to my next target.

Can I please just take a minute to thank the Internet? Seriously, without it and the teenage need to post provocative pictures of oneself online, this whole Clovergate thing might not have been possible!

I met up with Vicki later in her AP Zoology class. I was shocked she took that class too—totally threw me for a loop. Was she researching different animals to sacrifice?

I sat down in front of her; she glared at me like a wolf. That also threw me for a loop, because she tends to make the same face whether she's happy or mad.

"Can I help you?" Vicki asked.

"I was just Googling '*Satan-worshipping cults,*' a hobby of mine, and I came across these," I said, and shuffled through the photos. "Check these out! Is that you with the whip in your mouth? And in *this* one, you're riding some guys. Neat! What about this one? Is that a goat, or has Lucifer arisen and I just wasn't told about it?"

"Why are you showing me these?" Vicki asked. She played *I don't care* very well.

"I'm just trying to protect you, Vicki," I said. "I would hate it if these were accidentally e-mailed to your mom. Does she still teach Sunday school at Brighter Baptist Church?"

Vicki turned bright red; she was so flustered she almost looked alive. She yanked the photos out of my hands. I gave her an evil smile she would be envious of and handed her a yellow flyer.

Back in the journalism classroom I put an *X* across Vicki's face and actually gave Malerie a high five.

Clovergate Day Two had been better than Day One! I felt chills, the kind of chills you get when someone supposedly walks over your grave from a previous life, but I knew these chills were telling me my Northwestern acceptance letter would soon be on its way.

Come to think of it, I don't think I even went to class today. Oh well, I'll just tell them I had the runs. That works every time.

Have I not mentioned my "the runs" trick? Oh, it's genius! Just tell your teacher or counselor that you were late or were absent because you had "the runs." It's specific, but vague enough that they don't ask questions.

They can't give you detention for having diarrhea. It's practically foolproof. What are they gonna say to you? *"I don't believe you, show me"*??

I don't endorse truancy or tardiness, but if you're ever in a bind (like trying to blackmail your peers in a week to better your chances of getting into the university of your dreams), it's a great tool. Word of caution: Use sparingly. Otherwise they send you to the school nutritionist and make you pee in a cup. Don't ask.

CLOVERGATE DAY THREE

Claire Mathews and Coach Colin were the only victims left. I'd saved the hard part for last; I wanted to stretch my blackmailing legs before running the marathon. (Did I really just say that? Who am I?)

I spent half the day just pacing in front of the Clovergate board. I knew what I had against them. I knew how to use it against them. I knew what I needed to say to them. But *how* was I going to say it to them?

"Hey, Carson," Malerie said to me. "Why isn't Justin Walker on the board? Or what about that one cheerleader who told everyone her boobs were real but then got kicked in the chest at a pep rally and had silicone dripping down her shirt? It seems like they'd be good candidates too."

"Don't worry, they'll be in the magazine too," I said. "If I can get Claire and Colin under my thumb, I should have control over all the other athletes and cheerleaders also."

"You're going to be so powerful," Malerie said. "Which is funny, because you've always reminded me a little of Margaret Thatcher."

"Thanks?" I said. I'm hoping it's because I also wear a lot of blue.

I gathered up my final two copies of the yellow flyer and headed out of the journalism classroom. I decided to start with Colin. He was the first faculty member I would be attempting to blackmail, so I was extra anxious.

I went out to the baseball field. Colin had just finished with a PE class.

(This is off topic, but I want you to do something for me. Put a picture of high school students roaming the yards during PE and a picture of inmates roaming the yard at a prison together. Look between the two. See the difference? No? BECAUSE THERE IS NONE!)

I took a deep breath and centered my thoughts. Imagining my first steps on the Northwestern campus gave me courage and I walked up to the young coach.

"Hey, Colin!" I called to him.

"Football tryouts are over, son," he said, not even making eye contact with me. Douchebag.

"No, thanks, I'd rather have paper cuts on my corneas," I said. "And please don't call me 'son.' You were a senior when I was a freshman, remember? I tutored you in biology."

"You're that newspaper boy, aren't you?" Colin said. "Did you come out here to interview me?"

"Nope," I said. It seemed best to strike quickly. "The *Clover High Chronicle* doesn't have a sports section, but the *statutory* section is free."

He dropped the bats and baseballs he was carrying.

"I don't know what you're talking about," he said. The way he was looking at me, though, like a venomous snake, told me he begged to differ.

"I think you do," I said.

He looked like his head was about to explode. I was happy he had dropped the bats.

"Are you accusing me of something, boy?!" he yelled, and stepped toward me.

I raised a hand, mostly to block the spit as he talked, but the motion silenced him like I was a Jedi.

"Let's not play the question game, shall we?" I said. "It's one sport I'll beat you at. I'll get to the point with this. I know about you and Claire Mathews and have a video to prove it. If I go public with it, you'll lose your job, your trophies, and your reputation, and you'll never be allowed back into this high school world that you clearly love so much."

Looking back at this moment, I probably should have approached him in a more populated area. Colin could have easily snapped my neck and buried me under the pitcher's mound. But instead of killing me, he just sort of retreated into himself and became quiet. It was kind of sad.

"What do you want?" he said.

I handed him a flyer. Was this dude gonna cry on me?

"I want you to be *there* at that time," I said. "I also want to recommend not sleeping with students— *strongly recommend.*"

I ran off, mostly in case he thought of killing me, and because my work with Colin was finished. I got back to the journalism classroom and Xed out Colin's picture. I had one more victim left! Just *one*!

It's really hard finding a moment when Claire is alone. She's like the Clover High Hillary Clinton. I must have followed her around campus the entire rest of the day. She doesn't even shit alone—she makes some of her cheerleading minions go with her to the bathroom. I've always suspected she doesn't wipe her own ass.

I didn't want to waste any more time. I ultimately decided to just write her a little note at the bottom of her yellow flyer, something I knew she wouldn't let others see.

How does it feel being the Walker boys' girlfriend? it said. I prayed she would notice the strategically placed apostrophe.

Later, after school, I found her and the cheerleaders practicing a pyramid in the quad. I walked up to her and subtly handed her the yellow flyer. Okay, I may have chanted "Two, four six, eight . . . heard you like to fornicate!" too. I couldn't resist.

"You dick!" she said. But her already big eyes grew even larger when she read the flyer. I guess the apostrophe worked! *The queen bee was my bitch now!*

I skipped back to the journalism classroom. The *Rocky* theme played in my head. The hard part was over! *I was almost there!* All I had left to do was tell the Clovergate victims what I wanted from them at the meeting on Friday.

I may not have any literary magazine submissions yet, but I have their attention, and that alone feels like a victory!

CLOVERGATE *DIA CUATRO*

If I thought the night I caught Nicholas and Scott was my birthday, today must be Christmas. So *Feliz Navidad* to me! You'll understand this Spanish madness in a minute, don't worry. . . .

Let me start this entry off by saying I've had a lot of morality issues since I started this whole blackmailing escapade. Even I, Carson Phillips, thick-skinned and virtually heartless, have a conscience. It started, of course, with Nicholas and Scott in the bathroom and has quietly been eating at me ever since.

Have these people made my life a living hell for the past four years? *Yes.* Do these people deserve being treated like this? *In my opinion, yes.* Am I a horrible person for doing this to them? *Maybe.* Is this the most selfish thing I've done to date? *Definitely.* Will the guilt I'm starting to feel outshine the greater good I'm trying to accomplish for the future? *Hopefully not.*

Am I a hero in this story, or am I the villain? Which

side is the author of my first unauthorized biography going to take?

I also worry about the repercussions constantly. What if I get caught and "blackmailing" goes on my permanent record? Will Northwestern accept me with a scarlet letter? If not, then I'll *really* be stuck in Clover forever.

This kind of thinking puts me in weird depressing funks and I wish I hadn't flushed those pills Mom got for me.

It's such a gamble, and the stakes are so high. But no one ever got anywhere by sitting still, and I keep reminding myself of that. What I'm doing right now may be selfish and wrong, but I'm doing it for all the right reasons. So that validates it, right?

I've always thought I'm going straight to hell, and after this week, I've pretty much cemented my fate. I'm sure Vicki will be there too; maybe I'll finally get her to write for me down there.

I just hope there's a *Daily Hell* I can write for. I could do witty editorials like "Hell: Hath It Lost Its Fury?" and maybe weekly updates on who is torturing whom. I'm guessing there will be a plethora of CEOs and politicians to interview. There won't be any religious groups to offend in hell, so I imagine I can write anything I want. Maybe it won't be so bad!

Wait—am I actually positively depicting *hell*? Whoa, I've had a rough week.

But then, after all these doubts and worries and macabre premonitions, a day comes along that makes me think God is on my side. Like he's sitting up in the clouds saying, "Here you go, kid, keep doing what you're doing!"

And today, *that* message practically came with a bright red bow tied around it. I'll explain. . . .

Since I had a lot of success passing out the flyers, I went to the teachers' room to make copies of a poster I made advertising the publication of the literary magazine. I may have been a little full of myself, but I figured I'd be so busy working on the magazine over the next couple weeks I wouldn't have time to make them then.

It's been two years since I taped over the lock on the teachers' room door and no one has noticed. I went to the copy machine and found a warning notice that had been put on it:

NO STUDENT USE ALLOWED.

Clearly, this was intended for me. I ripped it off and made five hundred copies; I wasn't going to miss a single corner of this school.

While I was waiting for the copies to print, I heard a loud commotion from inside the supply room around the corner.

"Quick, inside here!" I heard a woman's voice say.

"*¿Dónde está la estación de tren?*" a man said.

There's a small and awkwardly placed window that sees right into the supply room (which actually inspired my theory that Clover High used to be an institute for the mentally insane). I peered in through the window, and in between the shelves of supplies I could see Emilio getting it on with *Ms. Hastings! Mr. Gifford's receptionist!*

"I could get fired for this, and I really need that dental plan!" she squealed as Emilio kissed her neck.

"*Necisito tomar prestado un libro de la biblioteca,*" Emilio said passionately.

She slammed him against shelves of pens and staplers. It was kind of hot.

"It's normal for men to be with older women in

your culture, right?" Ms. Hastings asked, suddenly getting self-conscious.

"*Tenemos varias alpacas en la granja de mi padre,*" Emilio said.

Ms. Hastings grabbed his neck and forcefully kissed him.

"I have no idea what you're saying, but you are so hot!" Ms. Hastings said, and shoved his face in her breasts. "And young, and tan, and imported! I feel like I'm in *Eat, Pray, Love!*"

"*¡Por favor, pásame un pedazo de pollo frito!*" Emilio growled.

"Wait," I said to myself. *"Pollo?"* How was chicken brought up?

Ms. Hastings slapped him. "Was that dirty talk? I love dirty talk."

She slammed him against rolls of butcher paper. I was starting to feel sorry for Emilio—he was getting the shit beat out of him. Maybe my theory about Ms. Hastings was wrong; maybe her ex-boyfriend was the one who was hiding from her.

"You're so Spangalicious, I love it!" Ms. Hastings screamed.

Their breathing became louder and louder and louder, they pulled each other's hair, tongues were united—it was *Fifty Shades of Gringo*!

"Ms. Hastings?" a voice from outside the teachers' room said.

"*Coming!*" Ms. Hastings peeped. I'm certain it was a double entendre.

Emilio tried following her out the door but she stopped him from doing so and disappeared into the hallway. I wanted Emilio to wash his hands just so I could shake them. Even *I* needed a cigarette after that.

Emilio's cell phone rang. "*¿Hola?*" he said. He looked around to make sure he was alone. I ducked behind the copy machine. "Hey, what's happening, bro?" he said.

Wait a second, I thought to myself, *did he just—?*

"Nothing, I was just feeling up a receptionist," he said . . . *in perfect English*! "I'm one away from beating my record, man! This morning I literally put the 'dic' in 'valedictorian'!"

He looked up and saw me on the other side of the window. *El panic loco.*

"I'll call you back, bro," Emilio said.

We. Need. To. Chat, I mouthed at him.

I texted Malerie immediately. I figured I could use a hand with this one.

"I'm taking the PSAT," Malerie texted back.

"I'm tired of your excuses, Malerie!" I texted.

Ten minutes later, Malerie and I were in the journalism classroom, shining a bright lamp in Emilio's face. Malerie even had her camcorder aimed right at him. It was just like *Law & Order*, except not predictable.

"So, *Emilio*, how long have you been a *fornicating exchange student*?" I said, feeling clever. "And I would tune down the Telemundo. Malerie is in Spanish Four; she knows a fake Spaniard when she sees one."

"*Sí.*" Malerie nodded. "I'm also fluent in Celtic and Elvish. Now speak! What aren't you telling us?" Clearly, Malerie was back in character. "Is Emilio even your real name?"

Emilio sank into his seat and lowered his head in shame. "My real name is Henry Capperwinkle," he said.

I tried my best not to burst out laughing hysterically but my eyes watered and my shoulders pulsed up and down. *Henry Capperwinkle?!* Was he serious?! I'm laughing right now thinking about it. That shit is funny!

"I'm from San Diego, not El Salvador," Henry said.

"SeaWorld! I knew it! He smelled very faintly of dolphin," Malerie said, and pointed at him. "What else? Tell us the truth!"

I just stayed quiet and let her do her thing.

"The only Spanish I know is from level-one *Rosetta Stone*, which I stole," Henry said. "I've been saying the same ten phrases over and over again and no one seems to notice. The people here are total idiots!"

"Huh," I said. He made an interesting point.

"Please don't tell my host family," he said.

"But why would you do this?" I asked him, much more intrigued than resentful. You know me: I kind of respect anyone working the system to their advantage.

"Are you kidding? For just a couple hundred bucks a month I get food and housing," he said as his focus faded off. "And *girls*. Girls like nothing more than a guy who speaks a little Spanish. Just a little '*rrrrrrr*' of the tongue drives them crazy."

"It all makes sense now," Malerie said. "All those *Doctor Who* e-cards I sent you in Spanish—they meant nothing to you!"

"How long have you been doing this?" I asked.

"A couple years," Henry said. "It was a buddy of mine's idea. He goes to Lincoln High. They think he's Nigerian. The guy is white as rice but no one looks into it because they're afraid it'll seem racist if they do."

I just stared at him. I was totally impressed, but I wasn't going to let him know that.

"Dude, you can't blame me," he said.

"Yeah, I can," I said. "I can blame you *mucho.*" Luckily, I had one more yellow flyer left I had been planning on saving for a scrapbook. "This is for you, *si se puede*ophile."

After school, Malerie and I pinned Emilio's picture to the Clovergate board and put an *X* through it. Clovergate Day Four has been an unexpected success!

Yo soy un afortunado hijo de puta! Which, according to Google translation, means: *I am one lucky son of a bitch!*

CLOVERGATE DAY FIVE: THE MEETING

Today is the day: Make it or break it.

I couldn't sleep at all last night. I kept tossing and turning with horrid visuals of how this meeting could go if it didn't work out the way I wanted.

Anyone can have dirt on someone else, but how was I going to convince these people I had the means to use it against them? What if they all flat-out refused to cooperate? Would I actually expose the information I had on them? Would anyone else at school believe me? I'm not exactly Miss Congeniality.

I could start off by releasing one person's info, to see if it spread. Would people be more eager to participate if they saw one of their friends' lives ruined? Who would I use as the pawn? Was I capable of ruining someone's life? If I did that, was I any better than them?

My work was cut out for me. I had to persuade everyone I had an influence over the student body while also convincing them I was heartless enough to go public with their secrets—a very hard thing to do when you're the only editor of a failed school newspaper.

All day at school I had horrible pains in my stomach and chest. I was so nervous that I was afraid of getting the runs for real.

My eyes were glued to the clock all day. Finally the last bell rang and school was out. It was time.

I went into the journalism classroom and tidied it up a bit while I waited. I was so excited to be having guests in my classroom. It had never had more than seven people in it before. I even considered running out to the store to get some hors d'oeuvres but reminded myself this wasn't a party.

I made Malerie come to support me. She seemed more nervous than I was. She found a stool and perched in the corner of the room, watching everything through the side-screen of her camcorder.

It was starting to get late and the weekend was getting closer. It had been nearly an hour since school had ended, and not a single Clovergate victim had come.

Was no one taking me seriously? Was I even remotely threatening to them and their reputations?

Were they all together somewhere just laughing at my yellow flyers?

A few more minutes of worrying later, I realized I was giving my peers way too much credit. One by one, they all started moseying into the journalism classroom.

Vicki and Dwayne were the first to arrive.

"Well, well, well," I said. "It's about time." I was reserved and played it cool; I don't know where my calmness came from.

"Relax. We had detention," Vicki said.

Detention! All the victims had after-school activities; that's why they were who they were. I'd forgotten.

Claire was the next to arrive. She took one look at Dwayne and Vicki and said, "Oh no." The princess didn't like being in the company of peasants.

Nicholas and Scott showed up next. *Really, Nick and Scott? You show up together to a meeting where you're being blackmailed for being together?* But then again, I realized they're *always* with each other. How has no one put A and B together before? Worst closet-couple ever!

Remy was next to show up and was petrified to see

the rest of the school council. The council members all gave each other cordial nods, but it was still awkward, like when you see people you go to church with at Hooters.

Coach Colin came next. He and Claire didn't even make eye contact. *Smart.* (Take note, Nick and Scott! Now *that's* how you shamefully hide a spoon-buddy!) Colin was the only one to notice the Clovergate board. I'd forgotten to take it down.

Everyone was quiet. They gave each other looks like, *You too?* I could tell the question *What are they here for?* was eating at them.

Emilio . . . I mean Henry . . . whoever he is . . . was last. Everyone looked at him and then back at me. *Even him?*

I locked the door behind him and stood at the front of the classroom. My heart was practically jumping rope in my chest.

"Hello, everyone, and welcome to the journalism classroom," I said.

"You fascist!" Remy said.

"*¡Inodoro!*" Emilio said.

"Enough with the names!" I said. "Look, I'll make

this short and sweet. You're all here because I've got dirt on you."

They all groaned and huffed like a pack of bloated coyotes.

"I *know* why I'm here, and I'm pretty sure we all know why *Dwayne's* here," Vicki said. "But why are the rest of you here?" She eyed Claire creepily.

"That's for me to know, and the rest of you to never know, if all goes as planned," I said.

"This is bullshit!" Nicholas said. "Not to mention illegal! Do you know how many lawyers my family has? *Seven.*"

The rest seemed to agree with him.

"*¡Enséñame los pompones!*" Emilio said.

I had just gotten them here. I couldn't lose them yet.

"If any of you would like to *share* the information I have on you, please feel free to do so and leave the room," I said. The room went dead silent. They all looked at one another, each quietly encouraging someone else to go first. Luckily for me, they were all too proud to do so.

"I didn't think so," I said.

"I'm late for *Hello, Dolly* rehearsal," Scott said. "What do you want from us?"

"As you all know, I am starting a school literary magazine," I said, cutting to the chase.

"You want us to buy your school literary magazine?!" Claire said in a mocking tone. It pissed me off. Did she really think I had gone to all this trouble just to *sell* them something? She was the idiot for having sex with a coach, not me!

"No, Claire," I said. "I would never expect you to recognize an intelligent publication, let alone purchase one! But your friends and family? Yes! Why? Because you're all going to be in it. I want a literary submission from each of you!"

It was out in the open, and they all moaned like the whiny bitches that they are.

"So that's what this is all about?" Dwayne laughed.

"This is ridiculous," Vicki said.

"*¡Tu aliento huele a animales de la granja!*" Emilio yelled.

"Wait, I'm not even a student here," Colin said from the back.

"That's because I want something more from you," I said, and then pointed at Claire. "And you. I want a submission from every football player and cheerleader."

The room erupted in complaints. They thought I was out of my mind on some kind of totalitarian power trip. And to be fair, I was.

"*You* can't make me or my cheer team or anyone else do anything!" Claire yelled. She was so high-strung and high-pitched, I thought her head was gonna fly off her neck. "There's a reason why you and *Precious* in the corner over there are the only members of your club, and it's because everybody hates you. Even if you spread whatever *information* you have on us around school, no one is going to believe you, got it?!"

The others cheered her on and muttered their agreements. Scott did a solo round of applause. Remy nodded her head as though to the bass of a hip-hop track. Malerie kept looking behind her, trying to see where Precious was.

My posture started to slump. I'd been afraid this was going to happen. Their complaints got louder and louder and I fell deeper into my own self-doubt. It was happening, my biggest fear: They were realizing they outnumbered me and I couldn't beat them.

I could feel sweat forming on my forehead. They were all shaking their heads and rolling their eyes, mad that their Friday afternoon had been wasted. A few of them got up to leave the room...and that's when I *snapped*.

A rush of adrenaline surged through me and I was no longer vulnerable Carson Phillips. I don't know who the hell I was.

"*Sit down!*" I ordered. My voice was so sharp it scared them. They didn't know what to do but follow my instructions. I had the floor, and I had it *good*. Years of stomaching their shit had led to this moment and I went *Dante's Peak* on their asses.

"For years I have been poked and stabbed with your *bitchfork*, Claire!" I yelled with my whole body. I still don't know where the words came from. "You have beaten me down to the bottom of the high school food chain with the *shitty end* of the stick for far too long! You don't think they're gonna believe me? *I will make them believe!* You don't think the people at this school have just been waiting for an excuse to turn against you?"

Everyone's eyes grew to the size of whale testicles.

"Sure, they all hate me," I went on. "But that's because I'm the only person in town with an IQ larger than my shoe size and I don't hesitate to remind people of that! So go ahead and play all the mind games you want to with me, sweetheart. I'm not accepting that invitation to intimidation any longer. I have nothing to lose and a whole hell of a lot to gain, and this time *none of you are stopping me!*"

All the color drained from their faces. They were paler than the front row of the Republican National Convention. I had them, *I finally had them!* But I continued this impromptu performance. I went behind my desk and grabbed the first stack of papers I could find.

"Need some examples? Here are some examples!" I said, and started throwing the paper at them. "Poetry, short stories, essays, scripts, novels, *anything*! Write anything as long as it's in your words and in my hands ASAP! *Write about how much you hate me! Write in detail about how much you want to kill me!* Okay? *NOW GET THE HELL OUT OF MY CLASSROOM!*"

It's hard to remember what happened next with all that juice in my veins, but I do know they scattered out of that room faster than mice in a cat shelter.

A few minutes later, the Hulk-like alter ego slowly faded away and I came to my senses. My heart was still racing and sweat was dripping down my back. There's no way sex can feel better than how I felt at that moment.

"Malerie?" I asked in shock. "Did you *hear* me? Did you *see* me? That was incredible! *I did it!*"

There was no response.

"Malerie?" I said. I looked around the room, but I was alone. I'd even scared Malerie off; she had left with the others. Oh well.

I walked over to the Clovergate board and ripped off all the defaced pictures. I triumphantly wrote, *The Clover High Literary Magazine: Now Accepting Submissions* across it.

Northwestern, watch out: Next year Carson Phillips is coming…and he's *fucking crazy*!

10/24

I had the best dream over the weekend. I was standing in an elevator. It traveled higher and higher. I wondered if it was ever gonna stop.

I was older, not sure by how much. Everything was slightly darker than usual because of the designer shades I was wearing. I looked down and saw that I was wearing a snazzy tailored suit.

The elevator doors opened, and I was at the *New Yorker*.

Everyone freaked out when they saw me. I was confused by it at first. I had just seen my clothes so I knew I wasn't having a *naked-in-public* dream. I strode down a hall and all the employees cowered in fear as I passed. And then I understood it: They were afraid of me because I was their boss! I felt like Miranda Priestly in *The Devil Wears Prada*.

"I'm so sorry, Mr. Phillips, we weren't expecting you until noon," said Remy. She was alarmed and wearing a headset; she was my *receptionist*. "Should I move up your meeting with President Maddow?"

I sighed deeply. "I said I would be here earlier than usual. How was that not clear? An editor should be able to come and go as he pleases without being exposed to incompetence," I said.

I was *editor in chief* and I was an *asshole*. It was great!

"Mr. Phillips, here is your coffee, sir!" said Claire, running up to me with a steaming cup.

"Is this how I like it, Mathews?" I said, never making eye contact with her.

"Yes, sir," she said. "Fresh-ground Mongolian beans, with two teaspoons of Swiss cream, a cube of your favorite zero-calorie noncancerous sugar, and half a shot of Jack Daniel's."

"Thank you," I said to Claire. I took a sip and then immediately splashed the rest in Remy's face.

"I deserved that," Remy said. "Also, sir, your mother's home called. Apparently she's woken up from her coma."

I grunted. "Then tell them to up the dosage again. I'm paying them to keep her comatose," I said. Then I burst through massive double doors leading to my office. Remy and Claire weren't allowed to follow me in.

My office was as big as a small country. There were golden pillars and a grand piano. *I don't even play piano!* The walls were covered in honorary doctorates and pictures of me looking bored with enthusiastic presidents and prime ministers and Madonna.

I had floor-to-ceiling windows with the most breathtaking view of New York City. I somehow could see the Empire State Building, the Statue of Liberty, the Chrysler Building, Central Park, the East River, the Hudson River, Barbara Walters, and Times Square. I'm not completely knowledgeable about the geography of the city, but I'm pretty sure it was one of the only offices with a view like that.

My phone rang and I answered it. "Hello? Not now, Oprah." And I promptly hung up.

"Hello, Carson!" Malerie said, walking into my office.

"Hey, Malerie, how's my favorite publisher?" I asked her.

"Doing great!" Malerie said. "Your autobiography, *Clovergate: The Scandal That Started the Man*, is still number one on all the best-seller lists for the ninety-seventh week in a row! Do you think you have another best seller in you?"

I smiled and looked back at my view. "Always," I said.

And that's when I woke up. Well, the dream went on to include alien transvestites taking over the Earth and ended with me losing a game of limbo to Margaret Thatcher in a room full of ferrets, but I ignored all that.

While I don't think I could ever splash coffee on someone (or hang up on Oprah!), it was much more than just a dream: It was the goal. And if school today was any indication, that goal was a very possible future.

Claire and Colin must have gotten the word out to their armies of athletes and cheerleaders, because the line of disgruntled dipshits waiting to turn in their literary submissions was out the door after school on Monday.

"Claire said we can't cheer if we aren't cultured and is making us be in your magazine," said a cheerleader.

"Coach is making us write for you because he says we can't beat a team unless we can outthink a team," a cross-eyed football player said.

The submissions were rushed and short but it

didn't matter. Northwestern would see them and think I was inspiring students of all backgrounds to write! It was exactly what I needed!

I couldn't wait to get to Grandma's after school and tell her all about it.

∿

"So, I'm blackmailing the entire school to better my chances of getting into the university of my dreams," I told her as soon as I walked into her room. "And it's exhilarating! Who would have thought one of my greatest achievements would be criminal?"

"Get out of here," Grandma said with wide eyes.

"No, I'm serious!" I said happily. "I've been getting submissions all day from people—"

"No, get out!" Grandma yelled and pointed at the door. "Get out! I don't know you! Get out of my room!"

"Oh, no," I said. "Not today, Grandma. Please don't do this, not today—"

"Get out!" she insisted. "Nurse, there is a strange man in my room! Nurse!"

Grandma has these moments from time to time.

"Okay, I'm leaving," I said, and headed out the door. "See you tomorrow."

"Get out!" she yelled at me one final time. Even as I walked down the hall I could hear her yelling, "Get out! Get out! Get out!" from her room.

It's hard enough to see her every day and not have her recognize me, but to be considered a stranger by the person you love the most in the world is a different serving size of heartache.

I had been on cloud nine all day until that point. But the higher your cloud, the farther your rain falls.

I got home earlier than usual and found Mom on the couch (shocking!).

"You're home early," Mom said.

"Grandma is in one of her moods," I explained.

"Oh," Mom said. She usually looks guilty whenever I mention Grandma to her. "That's why I never go over there anymore; I can't bear to see her like that." She nodded along with her terrible excuse.

"*That's* why?" I said under my breath. The truth is, she doesn't like visiting Grandma because it makes her feel guilty, and that's one predicament she doesn't have a prescription for.

"How was school?" she asked me.

"Fine," I said. "I'm blackmailing the entire student body to better my chances of getting into Northwestern."

"Northwestern?" Mom asked.

"That's the place I'll be going to school at this time next year," I reminded her.

"Oh," Mom said. She looked down at the coffee table sadly. "I keep forgetting how old you are. I guess even my kid has to grow up."

Only my mother can frustrate me to no end and make me feel sorry for her at the same time.

"How was your day?" I asked her, although it didn't seem like she had had much of a day.

"It was fine," Mom said. "Judge Judy kicked a man out of her courtroom for not wearing pants and Ellen gave away free Xboxes to her audience."

"That's it?" I asked.

"Yeah, that's about it," she said in a melancholy tone. "Oh, and after Anderson I got the mail."

Why didn't she say so? There was a stack of mail on the counter and I immediately went to it. Butterflies were mating in my stomach as I flipped through the envelopes, but there was nothing for me.

It would have been ironic if I had been accepted already and I'd gone to all this trouble for nothing; there was still that chance. That would make a great story over cocktails when I was at my future neighbor's art show in downtown Manhattan.

Whoa, I've really got to stop making plans with fictional characters. It can't be healthy to develop relationships with people who don't exist.

I spent the majority of the afternoon wondering if I should include a "miscellaneous" section in the literary magazine. While I'm glad I'm getting more submissions every day I must say that teenagers are nuts; I don't know what half of this shit is. Is it poetry? Is it creative writing? Is it human?

One girl turned in an essay about how she's going to marry Justin Bieber one day and I think she's *dead* serious. Apparently she drives to his house every weekend and just stares at his home through the gate for hours.

Like, are you kidding me? Do you seriously think he's gonna walk outside, see you, and be like, "Girl, I've watched you watching me for months now and I think

I love you." *NO! You're fucking creepy! Drive your stalker ass home and stay there!*

Doesn't this make you wish parents slapped their children? Seriously, where are this girl's parents and why aren't they doing their job? Youth is not an excuse for insanity.

I'm putting this essay under "social commentary" for her sake. Crazy-ass.

A couple of hours later Justin Walker poked his head into the journalism classroom. He looked like a lost puppy and was carrying a single sheet of paper.

"Is this where I'm supposed to turn in something to your military magazine?" he asked me.

"It's a literary magazine, and yes," I said.

"Thank God. I've been looking for this classroom for hours, dude," Justin said. "I didn't even know this was here."

"I know, right?" I said sarcastically. "They should totally put numbers on the doors or something, right?"

"Or like a kiosk, like at the mall," Justin said. He looked around the room in awe. "Do you live here?"

"Practically," I said. He gave me his paper and I looked it over. It made Dr. Seuss look like Charles Dickens.

"Thanks, Justin, I see you wrote about trees…and grass…and how they're both green," I said.

Justin sighed and shrugged his shoulders. "Look, writing isn't my thing, okay? I'm not a west-brained person, so what?"

"Left-brained," I corrected him.

"What's that?" he asked.

"It's left-brained and that means you're creative," I said.

"Yeah, well, I'm not that either. I'm the opposite of left-brained," he said.

"So you're right-brained," I said.

"Yeah," Justin said. "I'm right-handed, too; that should show you right there."

"Yup, it totally should," I said. I gave up at this point. Sometimes for your own sanity you just have to agree with idiocy.

"Are you good at math and science then?" I asked, but regretted it right after. "That's normal for right-brained people."

Justin thought about it with a lot of effort. He looked lost in his own head, which is like a grizzly bear being lost in a studio apartment.

"No, I'm not really good at those either," he said.

"Then what *are* you good at?" I asked. I didn't mean it to sound the way it came out, but I'm naturally a prick, so it didn't help the situation.

Justin got really upset and threw his arms up in the air. "I know what you're thinking, because it's the same thing my counselor, Principal Gifford, and every college football recruiter thinks too. But I'm not just a dumb jock with bad grades, okay? There's much more to me than that."

I unreservedly nodded my head, to make up for causing him to feel this way. "Like what?" I asked him.

He looked at me like I had just asked him what the capital of Turkmenistan was. He didn't have an answer.

"Maybe you should figure that out," I said in the nicest way I could. "You've got to show the world who you are before it tells you, Justin. Otherwise you become victim to someone you're not."

It took him a while to catch on to what I was saying, but I could tell he got what I meant.

"Kind of like how I joined the football team to be the middle linebacker and now I'm the quarterback," Justin said. "I never wanted that pressure. I should have said something, but I didn't want to upset my brother. We still share a bathroom."

"Um…" I said. I didn't speak football; I was worried I might have ruined this guy for life. "Exactly."

"Thanks, bro," Justin said, and stuck a fist toward me. I dove halfway under my desk, afraid he was trying to punch me, but he just wanted me to bump it with my fist. After I did, his fist went through some kind of explosion and he made a sound effect to go along with it.

Did that mean I won? Was that a game? Why are athletes constantly playing games?

"See you at a game sometime?" Justin asked me on his way out the door.

I almost said, "I'd rather put my nut sack in a blender," but it's not nice to pick on people with special needs, so instead I said, "Maybe!" I tried to stop myself but couldn't halt the strong force compelling me to say,

"Oh! And Justin, keep your eyes open; the bathroom isn't the only thing you and your brother share."

I'm such an idiot. But we'd just had a moment—how could I not?

Justin once again thought really hard, and it took a lot of effort.

"Oh, man, you're not telling me..." he said, looking absolutely heartbroken.

"You didn't hear it from me!" I said. *Shit! I really stuck the fork in my eye this time!*

"Those *Nikes* are *vintage*," Justin yelled. "I told that jackoff not to wear them! I'm gonna kick his ass." He stormed out of the classroom.

I exhaled with relief. Me and my big mouth. Why am I always a hair away from sabotaging myself? I wonder how much I could get done if I wasn't in the way.

I'm a feeling a little mortified this afternoon. Some jock came in earlier and turned in a submission for the magazine. I thought it was a cute and innocent poem about his dog, but after some further reflection I'm convinced it's actually about his *dick*.

Gross. Oh well, I'll let you be the judge. It's still going in the magazine; I can't afford to be picky with the selections. I'm running out of time to put this thing together and send it off to Northwestern with a new application.

Remy also came in today to drop off her submission. I swear that girl grinds my gears more than anyone else at this school. Just the way she walks, like she's the smartest thing on the damn planet, annoys me. *Not in my classroom, Bilbo.*

"Here's a short story for your stupid magazine," she said with a gigantic eye roll.

"Thank you, Remy," I said. I didn't even say something witty back to her. After blackmailing virtually everyone I know, I've tried turning over a new leaf today. I'm trying to be as cordial as possible to the people I've victimized. (I think I have permanent bite marks on my tongue because of it.)

"I really have much better things to be doing with my time, you know," Remy said.

"Like finding your *precious*?" I couldn't help but say. I said I'm *trying* to be cordial; I'm not fully committed.

"Very funny, jackass," Remy said and handed me her short story. "It's not exactly my best contribution to the world, but it'll do. I'm just glad your magazine isn't going anywhere important. I'd hate to be the girl remembered for writing a mediocre short story."

"I'm so glad I caught you in a cheery mood," I said.

I looked it over. I could tell she had actually put a little effort into it. Remy always reminds me of myself that way, a perfectionist to a fault.

"And how exactly do you want to be remembered?" I asked her. "Or is this whole uptight-bitch image what you're going for?"

"I'd like to be known as a girl who didn't waste her

time," Remy said with a really dirty look. "I've never understood you, Carson. We've always been so much alike. You work just as hard as me, we get the same grades, but what do you do it for?"

"And *this* was wasting your time?" I said. "Looking inside yourself and creating something original and unique and completely from your imagination was a waste of time for you? Well, then I guess that right there is what sets us apart."

"Whatever," she said, and walked to the door. "I've got to get back to yearbook. Memories don't create themselves."

"Actually, they *do*," I said, and looked at her like she was crazy. "But I suppose you want everyone to remember a hypersaturated version of you."

"Forgive me, but I like keeping track of my achievements, okay?" Remy said. "Someone's got to." I think she had shown a tad more desperation than she wanted to. Good thing we aren't friends, otherwise I might have asked what she meant by that and would have been stuck there for hours listening to her mommy and daddy issues.

"You know, Remy," I said, "if you overachieve yourself to death, you'll never know what your real accomplishments are."

She made a nostril-clearing sound and left the classroom.

I got to thinking about things after Remy left. In ten years . . . not that I care, but I wonder how people will remember me. Will they remember me as that annoying kid from journalism who busied himself with meaningless tasks to validate his existence? Or will they eventually see me as that driven kid who tried his hardest to accomplish his goals?

Will they look back and remember high school as the greatest years of their lives? Or will they look back and remember all the people they hurt and trampled over for status?

If you put an American history book and a British history book together, I bet their descriptions of the 1770s would be very different. And if you took Remy's yearbook and a yearbook I would make and put them together, I bet they wouldn't even seem like they belonged to the same school. I guess there is no such thing as history; it's all just a bunch of common perception.

Speaking of perception, I showed that poem to Grandma after school. Although she still doesn't know who I am, she totally agreed that it was about a penis.

10/26

It's Friday and I had the misfortune of sitting through another student council meeting after school. *Don't be jealous.*

"We still need a venue for prom," Claire said, addressing her court of jesters. "I was thinking Quail Gardens?"

"What about Motel 6 up the highway?" I said. "I mean, everyone heads up there after prom anyway. Am I right?" I laughed at my own joke. Not sure who I was playing that one to—it's not like I've ever had an audience with these people before.

"Any objections to Quail Gardens?" Claire asked, therefore ignoring me. No one had any other ideas.

"Isn't Quail Gardens right in the middle of the country? And prom is usually at the beginning of summer, so everyone would be eaten alive by bugs," I pointed out. "I think the Clover dining hall would be cheaper and a lot smarter."

I wasn't just trying to be opinionated. When I was a sophomore, the seniors held their prom at Quail

Gardens and I heard complaints about the bugs. When all the pictures were developed it looked like a really corny sparkle effect had been added to all the photos, but in fact the "sparkles" were just gigantic gnats Quail Gardens was infested with at the time.

"The Clover dining hall it is," Claire said with a heavy sigh. "We need a theme."

"What about a fairy-tale theme?" Remy said, jumping on the chance to pitch it. "We could do a really easy Cinderella setting for the photos."

"Oh my God, I love Rapunzel!" Scott said.

You know me, I couldn't resist adding my voice to the topic.

"I'm not sure all the students would appreciate that theme," I said. "Like the *male* ones. You should do an era theme, like the Roaring Twenties or something."

They all looked at each other silently, hiding their objections.

"Twenties is fine," Claire said.

"Super," Justin added.

I finally got what they were doing, and it was annoying.

"Why are you guys letting me make all the

decisions?" I asked. "It was a lot more fun when I got to argue with you."

"Are you going to make us write more if we do?" Nicholas asked cuttingly.

"Speaking of which," I said, "the magazine is coming along nicely. I'm just waiting for a few more submissions." I eyed Claire, Nicholas, and Scott.

"Agnes Saunders, one of the ladies who works in the kitchen, is retiring next month," Claire said, changing the subject. "We were given fifty dollars to get her a retirement gift. I was thinking some new mixing bowls or maybe a nice toaster oven?"

"That seems nice," Remy said.

"Maybe throw in a rack of spices," Scott suggested.

"You're giving a woman who has spent the last forty years of her life making school lunches *cooking supplies*?" I asked in disbelief.

"It's appropriate," Nicholas said.

"It's like giving a dead horse new shoes," I said bluntly. "Treat her to a spa day or something she'll enjoy and that won't remind her of all the worker's comp forms she's probably had to fill out over the course of her career."

"Fine, lunch lady spa day, noted," Claire said, aggravated.

I don't know why they're always so annoyed with me. They should be thankful I'm here to tell them how stupid their ideas are.

"Monday, November fifth, we have a meeting with the principal and the superintendents after school," Claire said, concluding her checklist. "They usually have these meetings when they're about to enforce new campus rules."

"My brother had one of those meetings when he was in the student council," Justin said. "It was when they put a ban on see-through backpacks."

"It should be painless if we all agree to just smile and listen," Claire said.

Everyone turned and scowled at me.

"I'll be on my best behavior," I said. Jeez, tough crowd.

10/29

So, I was sitting at my computer in the journalism classroom after school (I got a head start on typing up the magazine submissions) when Dwayne walked in. Instantly the classroom smelled like a Bob Marley concert.

The fumes coming off that boy made me want to take him in for a human smog test.

"*Duuude*," Dwayne said, taking way too long to pronounce a one-syllable word.

"*Yeeesss?*" I said, matching his timing.

"I wrote, man," he said. "I wrote for you!" His eyes were so squinty he looked like he was sleepwalking. He handed me some kind of pot-influenced essay.

"Thanks, Dwayne," I said. Even the paper smelled like weed.

"You're welcome, dude. Thanks for busting my balls, man," he said. "I really enjoyed it."

"Come again?" I asked. I don't know why I was trying to make sense out of someone senseless.

"You really opened my eyes, man," Dwayne said

with his eyes closed. "You know, this whole writing thing, it's kind of nice. I mean, when do we really get a chance to *write* in school, you know what I mean?"

I did a double take. Was he serious?

"What about in *journalism*?" I asked. "I've been trying to get you to write something all year."

"Oh yeah," he said. "I guess I never considered that writing. I guess I always considered that *wronging*." He then burst out laughing hysterically. "Get it, man? Just like your homecoming float said! Anyway, dude, it was a trip. A total escape."

"Ah," I said. "Well, if you thought writing was a trip, you should try *reading*, Dwayne."

"Reading, huh?" Dwayne said. "I've never really been much of a reader."

"I understand," I said. "But did you know there's a difference between reading and *reading*?"

"Whoa, there is?" Dwayne asked, and his eyes half opened.

"Oooh, yeah," I said, completely messing with him. "You should try it. Anyone can read a book, but very few can *read* a book. Authors may write *these* words, but really mean *those* words. You know what I mean?"

"Dude, I'm tripping out right now. I never thought about that," Dwayne said, and rubbed his face so hard I worried it would come off. "I'm gonna go to the library and rent some books! They've got one here, right?"

"They do," I said. "And just to let you know, there are all kinds of ways to escape out there if that's what you're looking for. *Healthy ways*. And most of them don't cost any brain cells."

Dwayne looked off into space for a second, which I think means he was thinking about what I said, or maybe the mother ship was sending him a departure signal.

"Cool, man, I'll see you later," Dwayne said, and left the classroom. Well, he ran into a wall first and then left the classroom. Dumb-ass. Why do I feel like he'll be running for president someday?

It still smells like Cheech and Chong's house in here. I think it's starting to give me a headache. And why am I starving all of a sudden? I would kill for an ice-cream sandwich right now.

I've been really trying to work with Malerie this week. She wants to be published in the literary magazine so bad, but she's having trouble turning in a story that's, well, written by her. So every day after school, she and I have sat in the journalism classroom and gone over options.

"All right, what about this one?" she said to me, pulling out a few pieces of paper from her Hello Kitty binder. "It's about a creepy pedophile living in a candy factory with dwarf slaves."

"This is *Charlie and the Chocolate Factory*," I said, after reading the first five words.

"Oh…" she said, disheartened. "Okay, I've got another one. It's completely original. There's this orphan who doesn't know he's magic until a giant hairy man brings him to a magical place called—"

"Hogwarts?" I asked.

"How did you know?!" she said with eyes so wide they almost fell out of her head. "You must have already read it!"

"Me and three billion other people. That's *Harry Potter*, Mal." I broke the bad news to her.

Malerie shook her head; I've never seen her so frustrated. She looked up at me with a very serious expression.

"Carson, can I show you something I've never shown anyone before?" she asked.

"You're gonna stay clothed, right?" I said, a bit afraid.

Malerie looked around to make sure no one was watching. She even turned off her camcorder (which I wasn't aware was on). She reached into her backpack and dug around for something.

"This is something I wrote a long time ago," Malerie said. She finally found what she was looking for and handed me a copy of *The Hunger Games*. Yeah, you heard me correctly.

"This is a published copy of *The Hunger Games*, Malerie," I said. "You didn't write this, Suzanne Collins did. It says so right on the cover."

"That's what they want you to think," Malerie said. "During the 2004 Summer Olympics I went onto the website and wrote a comment. I said, 'These games would be so much cooler if the athletes didn't want to be here and were killing each other.'"

"Okay . . ." I said. It was a little concerning for many reasons.

"And then later, someone left a comment agreeing with me," Malerie went on. "They said, 'I couldn't agree more,' and that person was *S. Collins.*"

I rubbed my ears and blinked my eyes as hard as I could, making sure I was actually hearing and seeing this.

"Malerie, are you telling me Suzanne Collins created an entire book trilogy based on a twenty-word Internet comment left by a ten-year-old?" I asked, trying my best to translate what she was telling me. (I've become somewhat fluent in Malerian.)

Malerie closed her eyes and nodded her head. "It's been happening to me my entire life. When I was thirteen I used to send poems to my MySpace pen pal in England. She stole the poems from me and released an album with my words set to music."

"Really . . ." I said.

"Yes," Malerie said, and sighed. "And now that person goes by the name *Adele.*"

She looked at me with the most convincing eyes I've ever seen. Good thing Malerie isn't sensitive to facial expressions, because the way I was staring at her was just rude.

"But what about all those authors you copy who died before you were born?" I asked.

"I'm still trying to figure that out," she said. "Don't you see? You always thought I was the one copying people, but in reality, I've always been the victim. Please don't tell anyone my secret; I've been through enough."

"I can imagine," I said, and scratched my head. She flipped her camcorder back on.

"I'm glad that's all out in the open now," Malerie said. "I felt like it was the one thing holding our friendship back, and I didn't know how much longer I could keep it from you. I feel so relieved."

My head was spinning for a few minutes after that. I have to admit, the idea that Roald Dahl, J. K. Rowling, Suzanne Collins, and Adele were all stealing from a ten-year-old Malerie Baggs in Clover was the most interesting thing I had heard in weeks.

"Malerie," I said, "I want you to go home, pick

your favorite story that you or whoever wrote, and just change every other word. Change the genders of the characters, change the names of the cities, change the time period even."

"Why would I do that to all my masterpieces?" Malerie asked.

"Because if you do that I can publish it in the literary magazine," I said, and her face lit up. "When you do that, it becomes a *satire* of sorts, and those are perfectly legal. Usually some kind of social commentary and humor is involved, but these are desperate times, so I'll take your best shot at it."

Malerie jumped up with excitement. "That's amazing!" she said. "I've got to get home and get started!" She collected all of her things and headed to the door. "Thanks, Carson, you've given me back what has previously been taken from me." She paused dramatically for almost a full minute before proceeding out the door.

God, I hope the state supplies her with a good attorney one day and pray I'm never called in as a character witness. That trial is inevitable.

Later, on my way to my car, I saw Vicki sitting by

herself in the quad, listening to her iPod. I could hear the screaming vocalist from yards away. I hate to sound like a senior citizen, but *you call that music?!*

"Hey, Vicki," I said to her. "Do you have something for me? Something that could possibly be submitted to a literary magazine?"

She looked up at me with her trademark evil stare.

"Relax, before blood drips out of your ass," she said to me, and reached into her bag, which was sitting next to her. One of her fingerless gloves was pushed down a bit and I saw several marks on her wrist: *Vicki cuts herself.*

I couldn't help but gasp quietly to myself. "Vicki…" I said.

She immediately became super self-conscious and pulled up her glove.

"Here's my submission," she said, and shoved a paper into my hands. She got up and started to briskly walk away from me.

It was one of those moments when you want to help, but don't know how. You think of a million things to say but are afraid you aren't the correct person to say them. I knew I was the last person on Earth who should say something to her, but screw ethics, I did anyway.

"Vicki, wait!" I said, and walked after her. "Do you need to talk to someone?"

"Fuck off," Vicki said, and walked faster from me.

"Look, I may not be an expert on whatever it is that you're going through, but there have to be better ways of coping than harming yourself!" I said.

Vicki stopped and turned around to look at me. Her eyes were watery. I couldn't tell if she was more embarrassed or ashamed.

"You've got a lot of fucking nerve telling me how to live my life, Carson," she said. "It's my life—how I deal with my problems is my business, got it?!"

"Okay . . . I'm sorry . . ." was all I could say. She walked off, but I stayed standing.

I felt so sad for her (and I hadn't thought I was capable of sympathy). I also couldn't help feeling thankful I had never turned to something like that. No matter how hard things got for me, I don't think I'd ever see a solution in doing *that* to myself.

But who knows what she was really going through? Who knows what was really going on? You'd think after thousands of years on this planet the human race would have released some kind of handbook for teenagers, telling them how to get through *teenagehood* and get help for their issues. Yet here we are, struggling through it in our own ways.

It reminds me of something Grandma used to say whenever she would see a homeless person on the street: "There, but for the grace of God, go I."

10/31

I spent the majority of my Halloween bitching with the gays. (I've always wanted to say that.) I'll walk you through it. . . .

Once again, I wasn't invited to any of the Halloween parties after school. Not that I've ever wanted to go. After homecoming, dressing up isn't very appealing to me. I had way too much stuff to get done with the magazine anyway. I've got less than a week left and I've been hauling ass to get this shit done.

I had completely forgotten it was Halloween until Nicholas and Scott paid me a visit in the journalism classroom. They were dressed as Batman and Robin. And I'm not talking the dynamic duo from the horrible nineties movies, I'm talking full Adam West and Burt Ward from the sixties. I don't have gaydar, but *DING DING DING DING*!

"Wait, is this happening or did I fall asleep at my desk again?" I said as soon as they walked in.

"Very funny," Nicholas said. "It's Halloween, douchebag."

"Who are you dressed as?" Scott asked. "Gloria Allred?"

Nicholas and Scott looked at each other and laughed hysterically.

"Did you seriously just come into my classroom dressed like *that* and laugh at *me*?" I said. "I don't think you get to do that."

"Let's just turn in our papers and go," Scott said to Nick.

"Sounds great," Nicholas said.

They both resentfully handed me their submissions.

"Thank you, ladies," I said. I had no idea saying that would upset them so much. Nicholas practically threw a desk at me.

"That's not funny!" he yelled.

"He's not worth it, Nick," Scott said. "Come on, let's go get wasted off pumpkintinis at Claire's house and watch *Hocus Pocus*."

"You have no idea what you've put me through in the last week," Nicholas said, this time pointing at me. He was so worked up about it. Suddenly all that guilt I had sort of felt a few days ago swept over me.

They headed to the door, but before they left I shouted, "I'm sorry!" They looked back at me as if they had imagined it.

"What?" Nicholas said. I don't blame them for being surprised; I've only said those words like three times in my life.

"I'm sorry," I said again, making sure they heard me. "Ever since that night in the bathroom I've been thinking about things, and I really owe you guys an apology after all of this."

"I don't want to hear it," Scott said. "Blackmail me once, shame on you. Blackmail me twice, shame on me. Let's get out of here before there's a third time—"

"Look, I find it hard enough being at this school, and I wear my disgust on my sleeve," I said. "I never hold back anything, and it's still challenging. I can't imagine what it's like to keep something so secret on top of all that. If I added anything to the weight already on your shoulders, I'm really genuinely sorry, but you guys really helped me out by being part of the magazine."

They waited for a "but," but there was none.

"Thanks?" Nicholas said, still uncertain.

"That's nice, I guess," Scott said.

"And, just to let you know, I'm never going to tell anyone," I went on. "Scout's honor. I know how small-minded this town is toward me, and I'm not even a homosexual; I'm just brilliant." I chuckled, because I was slightly kidding, but I was the only one laughing. Their faces fell and they looked at each other sadly.

"It's not just this town—it's this world," Scott said. "I mean, besides San Francisco and West Hollywood, it's kind of a touchy subject everywhere."

"And *I* can't move to those places," Nicholas said. "My family would disown me if they found out. My mom was on the 'Yes on 8' board. It was her idea to put the happy cartoon family on those yellow signs."

"So you're basically suffocating yourself for people who are incapable of loving *you* to begin with?" I asked. "That seems like a waste."

Scott grunted and folded his arms.

"Yeah, we've heard all the catchphrases before," he said. "You know, it's really easy for celebrities and politicians to say that it gets better, but it's a bit more difficult for us in the real world, where kids are getting killed every day."

I had absolutely no right or grounds to say what

I said next, which is partially why I was so inspired to say it.

"Scott, that is the biggest load of crap I've ever heard," I said. "No one is saying it's going to be easy. It may be the hardest thing you ever have to do, and some may have to wait and plan much longer than others. But if your life is being ruined because you're living in an environment that doesn't accept you, and you don't at least *try* to move to one that does, then you can only blame yourself."

They went quiet. I love doing that to people. I didn't mean to be so preachy, but if you're gonna come into *my* classroom, you're gonna hear what *I* have to say.

"I may have no idea what I'm talking about," I said, a bit ticked off now. "But we're all a part of a minority waiting for a majority to pull their heads out of their asses."

I looked at the time—it was almost six o'clock. The afternoon had flown by. I swear, whenever I'm working on the magazine, I enter a time and space wormhole of sorts.

"Now, as much as I would love to stay on this soapbox all day, I have a senile grandmother I'd like to get to before visiting hours are over," I said. "Enjoy your pumpkintinis."

And that's when I pretty much kicked out the caped crusaders; first time I've ever had to do that to people in the journalism classroom. They made me feel guilty, sad, and annoyed in a five-minute span and I hate it when people make me feel anything I don't want to. I was ready to go.

〜〜〜

All the nurses at Grandma's home were dressed up in Halloween costumes, which did nothing to ease her comfort level.

"Who are you?" Grandma asked me when I first walked in.

"Your grandson," I said, wondering if she was going to kick me out again.

"Why are all these people dressed up in ridiculous costumes?" she asked me.

"It's Halloween, Grandma," I said.

"Oh," she said. "I've never liked Halloween very much. I don't like it when people hide behind masks."

"Tell me about it," I said. There it was: high school in a nutshell.

11/1

I practically tackled Mom today when she came inside with the mail. I know I'm being super paranoid, but if by the slightest chance I *was* accepted already I don't want to miss the letter.

Thankfully, I know I haven't missed it, because Mom's been really insistent about getting the mail lately; she must know how anxious I am. Usually she waits until the postman can't fit anything else in the box and rings our doorbell. Maybe she's coming around?

I searched through the mail as if the Hope Diamond was hiding under an envelope. There were only bills and tacky vacation ads. I really don't think I've been accepted yet, which makes my stomach turn just thinking about it.

Every day I don't get an acceptance letter means I have to make the magazine count that much more. This literary magazine has to be the best thing since spell-check or I'm screwed.

Thankfully, it's coming together. Emilio (or Henry . . . whoever he is) slipped his submission under the journalism door sometime today during school. I have no idea what any of it means; I just wish he would have at least copied and pasted it into a Word document rather than just printing out the web page from the online translator.

Oh well, beggars can't be choosers. At least this will add some ethnic spice to the magazine—some completely fake ethnic spice packaged and sold by Caucasian-owned businesses, but at least it'll be there.

I expected Claire to be the last person to submit something. I figured she would snoop around to see who had actually turned something in to me before going through with it herself. And, no surprise, my prediction was spot-on.

Ms. Self-Righteous strolled into the journalism classroom around a quarter after four today.

"Howdy," I said.

"Here's my entry for your magazine," she said.

"Great!" I said. "Is it about contraception?"

Okay, it was a cheap joke, but I couldn't resist. This really stuck a fork in Claire—she practically threw a tantrum.

"You know what?" Claire said. "It must really be

nice to have plans to journey out into the world, but some of us don't have that capability. Some of us are stuck here and have to make the most of it. So excuse me for wanting to have a little fun my senior year. It could be the last chance I get."

It was dramatic and to the point. I could tell she had practiced this defense before, but I doubt it was meant for me. I think this was what she had been telling herself.

She tried to storm out of the classroom, and I should have just let her go, but I've been so stressed out lately I guess I was looking for something to argue about.

"And why are you incapable?" I asked her before she got to the door. "Why are you stuck here?"

She looked back at me but didn't have an answer. I hate bringing up the past, especially memories I'm a little embarrassed to remember, but one really meaningful one involving Claire came to mind, as if it had been in my back pocket.

"Second grade, Mrs. McCoy's class, we all went around the room and said what we wanted to be when we grew up," I said. "I said I wanted to be a

Nobel Peace Prize winner and you said you wanted to be a—"

"Ballerina," Claire said. I was shocked she still remembered.

"What stopped you?" I asked her.

Claire had to think about it. "They all laughed at me," she said.

"But *I* didn't laugh at you," I said. I remember wanting to laugh, but I held it in. I guess even then I thought laughing at someone's dream was one of the cruelest things one person could do to another.

Claire went silent again. I could tell she was thinking about what I'd said, and hated it. Claire's biggest fear: someone like me in her head.

"In what grade do we stop believing in ourselves?" I asked. "In what grade do we just stop believing, period? I mean, *someone* has to be a Nobel Peace Prize winner. *Someone* has to be a ballerina. Why not us?"

She stormed out of the room. This time I didn't stop her.

"And I can't be the only one who gets that...." I said heavily to myself.

Young people and dreams are like baby turtles on the beach. The eggs hatch and they have to scramble to the water before the birds get them. We all have our sights set on water, but only a lucky few make it there unscathed. Life has a way of swooping in and picking off the forces and beliefs that motivate us.

I'm so glad this turtle managed to dodge the birds.

Okay, you know how you know you're out of your mind with exhaustion? When you metaphorically refer to yourself as a *baby turtle*! God, I need a vacation after all of this!

Once I get Claire's submission typed into my computer, the literary magazine will officially be complete, and I will be the proud creator of what must be the Eighth Wonder of the World!

What a couple of weeks it's been! Had I known when I started this project I was going to be so immersed in everyone's problems, I might have had stronger reservations. Seriously, when did I become all these people's therapist? I'm blackmailing these assholes, not *raising* them.

They can still go fuck themselves with the sharpest stick in the woods for all I care…but that's the thing:

Am I starting to care? Am I starting to see the shit-wads as human beings and not vicious life-sucking crustaceans now? Has blackmailing people turned me into a better-rounded person?

God, I hope not.

11/2

Malerie and I were hanging out in the journalism classroom today after school (I swear I am one pillow and blanket away from making it my official residence). We were going through piles and piles of "her writing" that could be submitted for the magazine. I'm still helping her out with this whole "satire" thing.

My cell phone started ringing, which is an odd thing since it's rung twice since I got it. (Usually it's just Mom asking me if I can pick her up some Midol and a box of Good & Plenty on the way home from Grandma's.)

"I just turn my phone off while I'm at school so I don't hear it not ringing," Malerie said.

Even more shocking was who was calling me. Honestly, it was the last person in the world I ever expected to hear from.

"Who is it?" Malerie asked.

"My dad," I said. I was so flabbergasted I almost forgot how to answer the phone. "Hello?" I said tentatively.

"Hey, Carson," he said. "I didn't mean to call you after school; I'm sure you're busy with your homework and so forth."

It was so weird to hear his voice. It felt a little like he was a deceased family member communicating to me from the beyond.

"Anyway," he went on, never pausing for air, "I have some really exciting news to tell you. I'm getting married! Her name is April and we're expecting a baby! You're going to have a baby brother!"

I almost *shat* my pants. Literally, the floor was almost covered in my *shat*. "You've got to be shitting me," was all I could say, hence the choice of words.

"Yes, we're very happy, thank you," Dad said. "Anyway, she wants to meet you, so is there any way you could make it over for dinner sometime soon? Say, eight o'clock tonight?"

I'm not crazy for thinking that this is a totally fucked-up situation, right?

"I'd have to think about it," I said. My head was spinning so fast I'm not sure if I even knew my own name.

"Please do—in fact I'd really appreciate it," Dad said. "Hope to see you soon!"

"Okay," I said, and got off the phone.

"What happened?" Malerie asked me.

I wasn't sure myself, so all I could do was relay the bullet points of what my brain was still trying to process. "Apparently my dad is getting married."

"Congratulations!" Malerie said, and raised her hand to give a high five. I didn't respond.

"I guess," I said. "He wants me to have dinner tonight with his fiancée and, well, *baby mama*."

"Are you going to go?" she asked me.

I didn't know. I hadn't even thought about whether I was going to attend this…*event*. "I'm not sure," I said. "Things are complicated between me and my dad because there is absolutely nothing between the two of us. Does that make sense?"

"Totally," Malerie said. "Things are awkward between me and my dad too. He doesn't really have a relationship with me, because he doesn't know I exist."

"Oh," I said. "Sorry to hear that."

She totally just *one-upped* me on the deadbeat-dad situation. Now I *really* feel like I have to go. Oh well,

I guess it couldn't be that bad. It'd be nice to have a meal that wasn't microwaved for a change, assuming this woman was cooking.

No wonder Dad came over to have Mom sign the divorce papers—that sneaky bastard! And I didn't think about Mom. How in hell am I going to break the news to her?

11/2 again

It's just before midnight and I'm back from what has to have been one of the most uncomfortable and awkward dinners in the history of mankind. I'm telling you, the Last Supper has nothing on this.

It started with me rehearsing in the bathroom mirror for almost an hour what I was going to say to Mom. The best way I could think of breaking it to her started with me saying, "Mom, you know that episode of *Dr. Phil* you saved?" So I figured the best thing for me to do was to just sneak out of the house.

I walked past the living room to the door as quickly and as quietly as I possibly could. Of course, the one time she's conscious at seven-thirty in the evening had to be tonight. To make matters worse, she was in the middle of watching one of those Lifetime movies about a woman suffering from domestic violence, so I knew she was already not in a good state of mind to hear this.

"Where are you going?" she asked from the couch.

"I…" It took me a while just to say that. "I'm going

to dinner with Dad." It still surprised the hell out of both of us.

"Why?" Mom asked.

"Um…" I said. This was the moment I'd been dreading. "Apparently, he's getting married."

It took a few seconds for Mom to process the information.

"Oh, really?" she said. "I didn't know that. Good for him." Her eyes immediately went toward the television, but I knew she wasn't watching it. Her eyes became watery as she held in whatever was building up inside her.

My own heart felt like it had fallen out of my body just telling her; I couldn't imagine what *she* must have felt like. Mom and I have had our issues, but no child should ever have to see their parent look like that.

"He wants me to go meet his fiancée, so that's where I'm headed," I said.

"Have fun," Mom said. "Get home at a decent hour . . . and all that parenting shit."

"Okay," I said. "'Bye, Mom. *Love you*."

I didn't want to leave her, but I was almost glad I wasn't going to be there for the rest of the night. I didn't want to witness how Mom was going to handle it. I knew it wouldn't be pretty.

I got into my car, did my series of tricks to get it started, and drove off hating the night before it had even started.

Dad texted me April's address, where they apparently had been living together for the last seven months. Way to drop a line, *Dad*.

Her house was in a really nice part of town. It was painted yellow with white trim and had a picket fence around the front yard. There was even a *welcome mat*. It completely threw me off. I had no idea what to expect.

I still don't know why this woman would have moved to Clover. Dad must have convinced April the suburbs were a good place to raise a child. Is there a gene in women that makes them all secretly want to be June Cleaver? Clearly, there was one in April.

I rang the doorbell, which was positioned on the stomach of a kitty-cat doorbell cover. It was weirdly sweet. It made the house seem like the kind of place you'd eat freshly baked cookies or get murdered in. You know what I mean?

"I'll get it, I'll get it," I heard my dad say. He opened the door. "Hey, Carson, come on in."

It was a little jarring seeing my dad for the first time in so long. His hair was much grayer now and we were the same height. We awkwardly shook hands, each afraid to grip the other's.

"Good to see you, buddy, thanks for coming over," he said, and showed me into the kitchen. Everything in the house was so clean and put together, it made Mom's house look like an episode of *Hoarders*.

"And this is April," Dad said. He referred to the woman standing in the kitchen. I had to do a double take; I couldn't believe what I was seeing. She was beautiful, with bright red hair and fair skin. Her eyes were big and bright, but in a really pleasant way, not in a substance-abuse way.

"Hi, Carson!" she said happily. "It's so nice to meet you."

"You too," I said, and shook her hand. "Are you by chance a trademark of the Walt Disney Company?"

"Huh?" she asked.

"He's joking. He's very sarcastic," Dad said.

"Oh, I get it," she said. "That's very sweet, thank

you." She put her hands on her pregnant belly and from then on I had a hard time taking my eyes off it all night. It was so weird to think there was a baby cooking inside there that shared DNA with me.

"Let's eat, shall we?" Dad said.

Dinner was mostly quiet, with short-lived small-talk topics. I couldn't stop eating—the food was amazing. I kept waiting for April to start talking to herself or see an imaginary animal walking around the house or something crazy; there had to be something wrong with her. Otherwise, why was she engaged to Dad?

"Your dad tells me you're quite popular at school?" April asked me.

I snorted. "No, I'm active but not popular."

"He's part of the Newspaper Club," Dad said.

"Actually, I'm president of the Writers' Club, editor of the school newspaper, and just started a school literary magazine," I corrected him.

"Well, check you out!" April said warmly. I hated how easy it was to like this woman. "You must get really good grades!"

"He does okay," Dad said.

"I have a four point two," I said, annoyed with him

now. He didn't know me well enough to know what my grades were. "I would have a four point five, but I tend to argue with the teachers about their lesson plans, so . . ."

"Do you play any sports?" April asked. I didn't even have the urge to throw up on her after she asked that question, that's how sweet she was.

Dad started laughing. "God knows I tried," he said. "We'd always go down to the park and throw a ball around, but he never showed any interest."

"Did we?" I said with a mouth full of food.

"I quickly realized I wasn't going to get the major-leaguer I was hoping for," Dad said. "He kind of threw like a girl."

And then I got it—Dad was pretending to be something other than the selfish asshole he had been my entire life. April might have loved hearing this bullshit, but I had had enough of it.

"Dad, we never did that."

"Sure we did—you just don't remember," Dad quickly shot back at me.

"No, I would have remembered something like that."

"He's just exaggerating," Dad said, looking straight at April, as if I wasn't in the room anymore. "He has this creative imagination. I think it's what makes him such a good writer."

"Dad, who are you pretending to be?" I borderline shouted at him. "You left how many years ago and I've seen you maybe *twice* since then?"

"Carson, you're young, maybe you don't understand." Dad said.

"You're right, I don't understand!" I said. "I don't understand how you could abandon your old family and act like everything is okay in front of the new one!"

April's eyes fell to her plate.

"Your mom was unstable," Dad said.

"Yeah, I know," I said. "And you left me with her. What kind of father does that?"

"Carson, I can only say 'sorry' so many times," Dad said. The funny thing was he had never said it once. I must have inherited that from him.

"Thank you for dinner, April. It was lovely," I said, and got up from the table. "But I have to go now."

I walked right past my dad, not even able to look him in the eye, and walked out the front door. It suddenly became very clear to me what that dinner had been; it was Dad's way of authenticating something with April. He had tried using me, and it didn't work.

Adults can really suck more than teenagers sometimes.

I was so mad it felt like I got home in a matter of seconds. I cautiously entered the house, not knowing what state I was going to find Mom in. She was passed out on the couch. Balled-up clumps of tissue were everywhere. She had obviously cried herself to sleep. She was also clutching a framed portrait of her, Dad, and me taken years ago.

I turned off the television and covered Mom with a blanket. It's amazing how many lives one person can ruin.

I just hope Mom is going to be all right once I'm gone. There's only so much you can do over the phone.

11/3

Well, the *Clover High Literary Magazine* is officially done! It really turned out pretty great if I do say so myself. It deserves a celebration, but the truth is, I'm not going to feel like celebrating until I get an acceptance letter with my name on it.

The copies going on sale at the school are being printed first thing Monday morning, but I printed a copy at home and put it in a special snazzy portfolio and sent it off this afternoon to the Northwestern admissions office with a brand-new application. It miraculously has plenty of time to get there, which leaves me feeling very impressed with myself; hopefully it'll be a mutual feeling.

I feel like I just put all my hopes and dreams into an envelope and sent it to a total stranger. I made another copy to keep in this journal, so I'll always remember November 3 is the day I completed the impossible!

I think I'll take tomorrow off, though. Even God rested on the seventh day.

THE 2012 CLOVER HIGH
LITERARY MAGAZINE

EDITED BY CARSON PHILLIPS

TABLE OF CONTENTS*

*Other submissions can be seen on the new
Clover High Literary Magazine Facebook page.

Janitorial Genocide

BY CARSON PHILLIPS

September 19, 2012

CLOVER HIGH SCHOOL, CLOVER, CALIFORNIA—
Due to the latest budget cuts made by the state earlier
this year, Clover High School had to lay off two janitors
and force one into early retirement before the school year
started. When asked about the unfortunate dismissals,
Principal Gifford had this to say: "We were very sad to say
goodbye to the members of our staff, but unfortunately, we
were left with no choice. Voters put that schmuck in the
governor's office, not me."

However, after further investigation, it appears there were
many choices made this year when it came to budgeting.

"We're so excited we get to play football this year
with brand-new uniforms and equipment!" said a football
player, who would like to remain anonymous in this piece.
The new gear is courtesy of the school. "We're number one
undefeated, and I'm glad the other teams we play against
this year will know that just by looking at our bling!"

According to a recent Google search, the average cost

4

of a typical high school football uniform can range any-where from $100 to $500, depending on the girth of the player. Given that there are at least forty players on the Clover High team, the amount the school paid could range from $4,000 to $20,000, which would have been an ample sum of money to keep three working fathers employed for a few months longer.

There's a major difference between "no choice" and a bad choice.

For more information on this matter, please visit the *Clover High Chronicle* Facebook page or e-mail the writer at CarsonPhillips@thecloverhighchronicle.com.

5

Small-Town Sex Scandal

BY CARSON PHILLIPS

September 26, 2012

CLOVER HIGH SCHOOL, CLOVER, CALIFORNIA—
Last Thursday afternoon, Mr. Armbrooster, a veteran
health teacher, was escorted off campus by school security.
He had been fired for quote "teaching sexual education
lessons with inappropriate objects," but the exact details of
these alleged lessons remained undisclosed.

When asked about the situation, here is what one
freshman girl had to say: "Mr. Armbrooster was a pretty
cool guy. So what if he used a Gumby action figure and
a jar of Play-Doh to teach about the female reproductive
system? Gumby kind of looks like a fallopian tube. You
can't deny that."

"We're not stupid," said a male classmate. "We know
the uterus isn't lined with Play-Doh—you'd have to be an
idiot to think that. All I know is that I got a B+ on that test.
Thanks, Mr. A!"

In fact, that seems to be the common consensus
among his students. When you compare the test scores of

6

Mr. Armbrooster's class with any other of the health classes at Clover High, you can see a major difference. The average student tests 20% better if they are subjected to Gumby and Play-Doh.

"Mr. A gets fired for using props in his class, but Mr. ***** sleeps with all his female students and gets tenure? That's messed up!" said a peppy school counselor who wishes to keep her identity a secret.

It's messy, it's not fair, and it doesn't make sense. I wonder what preschool toys Mr. Armbrooster would use to explain this situation to us.

For more information on this matter, please visit the *Clover High Chronicle* Facebook page or e-mail the writer at CarsonPhillips@thecloverhighchronicle.com.

The Overworked Princess

BY REMY BAKER

There was once a little princess who had several respon-sibilities. Her parents, the king and queen, put way too much pressure on her since they had troubles managing the kingdom. Although she was very beautiful and bright and constantly excelled in everything she did, her parents always thought she could do better.

Every day, the little princess would bring her parents examples of all the things she had accomplished that day, and every day they had a way of making her feel like it wasn't good enough.

"Look, Mom and Dad, I got an A in my peasant-appreciation class!" the little princess said.

"You're better than this," the king said, looking over the report.

"We'd be more pleased if it was an A+," the queen said.

The little princess ran out of the castle and into the forest and cried under a small tree, feeling like she would never be good enough. The tree magically came to life.

8

"Why are you crying, my little princess?" the magic tree asked her.

"Because I'll never be good enough for my parents," the little princess said. "I try so hard but they're never pleased."

The magic tree gave the little princess a magic book, full of photos of her accomplishments and her friends. "Here. Every time you feel sad, I want you to look at this book and remember all the good things in your life," the tree said.

The little princess looked through the book and instantly felt better. She dried her tears and went back to her castle. From then on, every time her parents made her feel small, she would look at the book and remember all the things that made her so great.

She kept the book for the rest of her life, well into her queenship, and shared it with all the princes and princesses who later became her children and grandchildren.

The End.

Creatures of the Darkness

BY VICKI JORDAN

It was a world of vampires and demons, where innocence was rare and so were the living. It was a world of darkness, where light had been outlawed and nightfall had swallowed us whole.

An epic war had been fought, and the creatures of the dark had finally prevailed over the promoters of the light. Finally, for the first time in existence, the people of the shadows could come out and freely walk among one another in the rays of a dying sun, which had once been used to shun them away.

A little girl, a child of the light, had survived the battle and crawled out from under the ashes of the destruction. She looked around at her altered world in dismay and confronted a vampire about the changes, of which she did not approve.

"Why did you turn my world into a world of night, and make wrong into a new form of right? How could you make all the light disappear, and with it everyone I once loved so

10

dear? Why are the shadows now the new sun, and why is everything lost what you have won?"

The vampire looked down at the little girl with amusement and delight.

"Because, little girl, this is the real world you see, where there's no light to shine on false identities. We didn't destroy the world just to scare; we simply uncovered what was already there. What has come out was all the darkness that was once hidden within, and you'll soon meet the darkness in you once my fangs pierce your skin."

We are our own greatest fears....

11

Top of the Pyramid

BY CLAIRE MATHEWS

Every Friday night at halftime my cheer team pulls off one of the most dangerous stunts in the cheer world. We call it the Cheermageddon.

Three pyramids are formed in a line. A girl on the top of the center gets jolted in the air and does a backflip while the two girls on the tops of the other pyramids flip underneath her, switching places before the center girl gets back.

While it's hands-down the best crowd-pleasing stunt we know how to do, it's also the most dangerous. I love being a cheerleader, but being at the top of the pyramid means you'll get hurt the most if you fall. Being the smallest girl on the team, I'm also the girl on the center pyramid virtually risking her life every week for the enjoyment of others.

It makes me wonder, would it be so entertaining if the crowd knew everything was going to be all right? Or are they all just secretly waiting for someone to get injured?

People are constantly put on pedestals in our society, sometimes for the wrong reasons, but mostly because

12

they're doing something or capable of doing something that no one else can. But do we give people that status just so we can watch them fall? Sometimes I think the worst thing you can do to someone is idolize them or make them out to be anything else but human; then you're only giving them room to disappoint you.

When I'm thrown up in the air every Friday night, for a split second I feel like the loneliest person in the world. I think, *Wow, no one can reach me up here.* And when the momentum is over and gravity starts to pull me back down, I'm so thankful to be on the ground again. I just hope the momentum never pulls me down too far.

13

The Color Green

BY JUSTIN WALKER

I like the color green. When I see the color green it makes me think of trees and grass. When I think of trees and grass, I think of football. When I think of football it makes me happy.

I know I'm not the brightest bulb in the knife drawer. People call me stupid, idiot, and a Neanderthal (even though I'm not from the Netherlands) all the time. But if the point of being alive is to find out what makes you happy, then I'm pretty much set. All I have to do is look at the color green.

So who's the idiot now?

I also like the color blue. When I think of blue I think of the ocean. When I think of the ocean I think of bikinis. When I think of bikinis I think about all kinds of things that make me happy, and they're not green!

At least I hope not. If they are, you should probably see a doctor instead of inviting me back to your parents' beach house. That's just gross and rude. Seriously, girl, you live at the beach—please shower more. You don't know what might be crawling on you.

14

Scott Thomas's "The Marquee"

I've always known that I was destined for fame. The image of my name in lights over the Clover Community Theater marquee isn't just a vision, it's a premonition.

If you're thinking, *But Scott, you're not* leading man *material—you can never be the star of something,* then I have two words for you, but since I promised myself I wouldn't swear in this essay, I have another two words for you: *You're wrong!*

There isn't just one cookie cutter in the shape of *stardom,* my friend; it comes in many sizes and colors. You just have to map out your own destination to it.

One day, I will produce, write, direct, and star in my own one-man show. It'll premiere at the Clover Community Theater, but the reviews will be so spectacular the show will go on the road. We'll hit all the major cities (except Chicago, because I can't risk the wind) and I'll gain a massive fan base.

I'll sell the movie rights to the highest bidder, maybe go on *Jimmy Fallon* and tell him how the dream all started, and after a long and luscious career I'll retire and punch

15

out a couple autobiographies, which will then be turned into massive Broadway musicals.

Ambition doesn't grow on trees, girlfriend. You gotta grow dem leaves yo'self.

Every day when you wake up, take the Scott Thomas approach to life. Imagine your own marquee with your own name in lights so bright you'd go blind if you stared too long at them. Imagine that marquee following you around wherever you go, letting the world know *you're there!*

Scott Thomas in Geometry! Scott Thomas in the Locker Room! Scott Thomas in His Car! Scott Thomas in the Bathtub! Live your life the way all the greats did, with your name contractually above title. Never be a sidekick to your own life!

16

Unstoppable Love

BY NICHOLAS FORBES

Roses are red,

Violets are blue,

No amount of money,

Can stop me from loving you.

Try as they may,

Try as they might,

I'm not letting go,

Without a fight.

Some say it's wicked,

Some say it's sinful,

Some say it's wrong,

And just awful.

I don't know much,

But when push comes to shove,

I definitely don't believe,

There's such a thing as wrong love.

18

My Special Little Friend

BY JOHN HARDY

You greet me in the morning,

Wanting to play,

Then stay with me hanging

For the rest of the day.

The same things stimulate us,

That's very true,

We spend time together;

Wish I had two of you.

19

You'll always be my best bud

Until the end,

Thanks for always being

My special little friend.

Call Me Isabella

A SATIRE, BY MALERIE BAGGS

A few years ago—never mind how short exactly—having little or no money in my Angry Birds wallet, and no sunscreen to go on the beach, I thought I would cruise about a little and be a total gangsta at the school.

It is a way I have of scaring off the freshmen and regulating the high school circulation. Whenever I find myself breaking out around the mouth; whenever it is a wet, cold September in my soul; whenever I find myself against my will looking at dead people, and bringing up the butt of every parade I meet; and especially whenever I lose a game of Hungry Hungry Hippos, that it requires a strong moral Principal Gifford to prevent me from deliberately stepping into the hallway, and methodically pulling people's pants off—then, I think it high time to get to the bus as soon as I can.

This is my price for being a gangsta. Like a philosophical flourish kitty cat throws himself upon his litter box, I quietly take the school bus. There is nothing shocking

21

in this. If they but knew it, almost all doctors with degrees, now or later, will eventually have to take the bus and have the same feelings towards the transportation system as me.

Also, there's a big whale I plan to catch.

Being Mrs. Bieber

BY HANNAH MORGAN

There I was, in front of Justin Bieber's house in Calabasas on a sunny Saturday afternoon. It was me and the usual twenty to forty girls who wait outside his home every weekend in hopes of getting a glimpse of him or a free private concert.

It was great: We were gabbing about Selena Gomez (who will always be known to me as "the other woman") and we blasted his music from a mobile iHome and predicted future Grammy nominations for his latest album, the usual.

But things got really tense when none other than infamous Renee Foster showed up!

"I believe you're in my spot, *Miss Morgan*," Renee said to me. Which was a total lie—everyone knows the twenty-eighth to thirty-first iron bars on the east side of his house's gate is *my* area.

"Oh, no, you don't, *Miss Foster*," I said. "You lost your spot when you abandoned J.B. for that immigrant Louise Tomlinson from *No Direction*."

23

All the other girls went "Oooo!" Renee so had it coming; nobody abandons my Justin.

"You didn't just insult One Direction in front of me!" Renee yelled. "I can be a fan of whomever and however many people I want!" She said it right in my face.

"Not at this gate, you can't!" I said, and bopped my head. She made me so mad I almost took off my homemade "Forever" earrings and tackled her ass.

"Hey! This is a private residence, not Disneyland!" said a guard up at the house. We all ran to our cars before they called the police on us again. Good thing, too, because I would hate for Justin to see me get into a physical altercation with Renee.

A few of the girls and I jumped into my Jetta and took off. "Let's go stand outside someone from *Glee*'s house now," one of them said.

Sure, I can see why some people may think it's strange that I drive to his house every weekend and wait outside the gate just to get a glimpse of him, but think of what a romantic love story it'll make one day.

24

10 Reasons Why Emilio Is Great

POR EMILIO JORGE LÓPEZ

1. Emilio tiene el pelo magnífico como un gallo.
2. Emilio huele como un perrito.
3. Emilio es el frijol en tu pupusa.
4. Emilio es tan suave como un conejo.
5. Emilio es lo picante en tu desayuno.
6. Emilio es un gran aventurero como una ardilla.
7. Emilio tiene la fuerza de un toro.
8. Emilio puede saltar alto como una rana sin miedo.
9. Emilio es el tocino en tu ensalada.
10. Emilio es el mejor amante que jamás hayas conocido.

25

3-D Lives

BY DWAYNE MICHAELS

So this whole 3-D thing has really taken over the world and I am loving every minute of it. I went to the movies last summer and saw *The Avengers*. I forgot to put my glasses on until like three-quarters of the way into the movie but suddenly I'm like screaming, "Whoa, Robert Downey Jr., why are you in my lap, man?!" It was trippy, dude!

That was an excellent time to have the glasses on. I mean, think about it, we put the glasses on and suddenly we're like, "The dude in the movie is throwing things at me, this is so awesome," because we know all we got to do is *take them off* and they'll stop throwing things, you know?

But then when we're in real life and people start throwing things at us, we're like, "You suck man, who the hell throws things anymore!?"

I know this may be too deep, but what if we took those glasses with us everywhere? Sure, you might get a headache but whenever there are things you don't want to be tossed at you all you got to do is take your glasses off, man!

26

Why do people live 3-D lives, when they could live 4-D lives all the time? Just wait for 5-D, man, it's gonna be so rad. I'm gonna be like, "Hey, Robert Downey Jr., wanna go grab a beer?" And he's gonna be like, "Yeah man, I do." And then we will, dude. We will.

11/5

So remember that meeting we were going to have with the principal and the superintendents? That was today. Remember how I promised to be on my best behavior and just sit there and smile? Well, I lied about that.

We were waiting in the middle of the auditorium at a table for almost half an hour before the principal and the two superintendents from the Clover Unified School District office showed up. So after that and everything this weekend with Dad, Mom, and finishing the magazine, I was already in a bit of a mood, I'll admit it.

"All right, let's get started," Gifford said, and sat at the head of the table. The superintendents each took a seat on either side of him. "I've called you here today to announce a new district rule that myself and the other principals in the district feel very strongly about."

Everyone had wide, eager eyes and gave respectful nods. My posture slumped a bit more out of spite.

"Starting next semester, all book covers, backpacks, and clothing displaying logos or writing of any kind are strictly forbidden," Gifford said. "So as council members, it's very important that you honor this rule and show leadership by following it."

The other student council members did a pretty good job of hiding their frustration with this news, but I could tell it was upsetting even to them. Even Remy was silently shaking her head.

I waited for a moment, making sure no one was going to say anything, and then I proceeded to flip the fuck out.

"Okay, agreed," I said. The superintendents were shocked I didn't raise my hand before speaking. "I hate some of the obnoxious and degrading things I read every day. And if I see one more person wearing one of those shirts that says I DO MY OWN STUNTS, I will physically rip off my face and throw it at them, but how are we supposed to learn and grow if you people keep taking away our basic rights of self-expression?"

Everyone's heads slowly turned to me in absolute horror, *Exorcist* style.

"Tell you what, buddy," Gifford said, without a

doubt counting to ten in his head. "Why don't you let *us* worry about student suppression?"

Claire nodded so hard her head almost fell off. Maybe she could live with being a kiss-ass, but I wasn't going to sit there and have my rights taken from me.

"Yeah, you people must know what you're doing since more students are stressed, depressed, and dropping out than ever," I said. "So you're doing a *real* great job with the decisions."

"You're out of line!" Gifford said, raising his voice. I could tell the lady helping him count in his head was starting to fail him.

"And you're on a power trip!" I said, matching his volume. "How does banning logos do anything but help your own conservative agendas?"

"Carson, please stop talking!" Claire whispered to me. I thought she was going to explode.

Gifford turned a shade of red I didn't know was possible for humans to turn. He knew I was right— they all did—and it embarrassed the hell out of him.

"This discussion is over. You will follow the new rules," Gifford barked at me. He looked from side to side at the superintendents. "And furthermore, due to your disrespectful attitude, I hereby revoke all off-campus student privileges for the rest of the school year. Your peers can thank you for that, *little man.*"

He was the second adult this week to use me to show off.

"Let's go, guys," Gifford said to the superintendents, and they strolled out of the auditorium.

I have never seen the student council look at me with such hatred before. Anger was practically melting out of their faces. Some of them couldn't even look me in the eye. Remy was almost in tears.

"They can't punish a whole school for one student's big mouth!" Justin said, getting up and kicking a chair over.

"I can't believe you all just sat there!" I said.

"Are you putting the blame on us?" Scott said, appalled.

"Thanks to you we're going to have to have prom in the cafeteria," Remy said, livid just hearing herself say it.

"We'll be spending a lot of time there, since we can't go off campus to eat anymore," Nicholas said.

"If you could write an apology letter to them,

maybe they'd reconsider?" Claire said, shaking. She was in full-blown damage-control mode.

"He should apologize to the whole school," Scott added.

"You're right!" Remy said.

"Yup," Nicholas said. "What about next week at the assembly?"

"Oh, Carson," Claire said shaking her head. "You always thought you were so much better than us because we all couldn't stand you, but get ready for *pure hatred* coming your way. As soon as the rest of the school hears about this and they tell their parents, the entire town will actually *hate you*!"

I couldn't believe what I was hearing. I was the only one who'd tried to stand up for the school and they were mad at *me*?! They were all going to hate *me*?!

"*All right, enough!*" I yelled. "I wasn't just standing up for myself in there—I was standing up for all of you! From the minute you guys walked onto this campus you were labeled as high school royalty, and you'd rather maintain that label than—*heaven forbid*—stand up for yourselves. Well, high school *ends*! And for your sakes, I hope you aren't the walking clichés everyone thinks you are, because life is going to walk all over you! It's going to bite you in the ass!"

I grabbed all of my things and stormed out of there as fast as I could. I was sick to my stomach. I was sick of them, of my parents, and sick of this entire town. I was just fed up with the whole world.

I drove straight to Grandma's and had a bit of a breakdown.

"I just don't get it," I told her, trying my best to hold back tears. "Why do some people have to work so hard for the things they want and others don't? Why are some people selfish by nature and some of us are selfish just to survive?"

She was busy knitting and didn't show much interest in what I was saying. But I didn't mind. I just needed to say these things; I needed to vent to another human being, even if I was talking to an empty house.

"You know, I told myself a long time ago that I didn't need anyone," I said, not able to hold back the tears any longer. "But lately, Grandma, I've wondered if I was wrong. I've always been one hundred percent independent, and it's such a hard thing to be sometimes...."

"Did you say something?" Grandma asked me.

"No," I said, and wiped away my tears.

"I'm making this for my grandson," Grandma said.

"What is it?" I asked.

She held it up. It was lopsided and made of many different patterns and colors of yarn. Clearly, Grandma had had different ideas of what it was every time she sat down to work on it.

"It's a *scarf blanket*," Grandma said.

I couldn't help but laugh. Indeed, it was. Even with Alzheimer's, she always had a way of making me feel better.

12/12

Well, the magazine has been on sale for a month and I've only sold one copy. And that guy just ripped it to shreds right in front of me. I guess Claire was right about the whole town hating me. I've been getting really dirty looks lately, much dirtier than usual. *Hateful*, I should say.

Yes, it's been a rough few weeks. I don't know why it's bringing me down so much; I've always thought everyone hated me. Careful what you wish for, I guess?

Still haven't heard from Northwestern. That's still a big question mark in my mind and a lump in my throat. I *really* need to get out of this town now.

December 15 is three days away. So in less than forty-two hours I'll know if I've been accepted early. Fingers crossed! At least I have that to look forward to.

I haven't really bothered doing anything with the *Chronicle*. I've just been reprinting old issues from September. I haven't been in the mood to write much lately; hence the month between journal entries.

Never thought I'd be at a loss for words....I guess life surprises you.

3/12

It's been a couple of months and I have nothing good to report, I'm afraid. Needless to say, I never got an early acceptance letter. But I never got a rejection either, so I've been waiting in a daze for these last few weeks, hoping my literary magazine did the trick. I think I'll forever remember today, March 12, as the worst day of my entire life.

I was sitting in my English classroom taking a final on *Hamlet* when Ms. Sharpton called me into her office to tell me that my life was about to become a tragedy of its own.

"Hi, munchkin, have a seat," she said to me. I could tell whatever she was about to tell me wasn't going to be good news.

"Oh no," I said, still standing. "Don't tell me.... Please don't tell me...."

"Just have a seat," she said.

I didn't want to sit. I felt like sitting would only allow the news to be real. If I didn't sit, then whatever it was (even though I knew what it was) wouldn't have to happen. I eventually sat down. My heart was pounding and my hands were trembling.

"I heard back from Northwestern today," she said. "Not good news, I'm afraid. They aren't letting you resubmit an application with your literary magazine. Apparently you missed the confirmation deadline, so your acceptance was denied."

"I'm sorry, can you repeat that?" I said.

"They won't let you reapply," she said. "You were accepted, but you never confirmed, so you were denied."

I was sure my heart would stop beating after hearing this. It was such a blow, such a mistake. Surely mistakes like that weren't made in real life.

"No, it must have gotten lost in the mail—I checked every day," I said. "Please, you have to tell them that."

"I'm afraid I can't do anything more for you," Ms. Sharpton said. "But you can always go to your second-choice school."

"There was no second choice," I said. I never planned to fail, so I've failed to plan.

I just wanted the world to rewind. I wanted to go back to the moments before she called me into her office, when I was miserable for superficial reasons. Now I felt as if a family member had died and taken a part of me with them; I was mourning my future.

"Well, you can reapply again after you complete your GE credits," she said, trying to cheer me up. "Clover Community College is still accepting applications. Would you like to fill one out?"

And now salt had been added to the wound. Not only was my spirit crushed, but now my soul would have to suffer through one or maybe more years of staying in Clover. I couldn't have imagined a more disappointing scenario.

"Carson, would you like to fill out an application?" Ms. Sharpton said.

Her words faded away. I was distracted by a postcard of the ocean on her desk. It seemed so peaceful and serene. I had never seen it in real life before.

"Carson?" she asked me.

"You know, I've never seen the ocean," I said.

"What?" she asked. "What does that have to do with anything?"

I got up and left her office and just walked for a bit. I must have walked around campus for hours just thinking about things. Northwestern had always been part of the plan. It had always been my next step. As worried as I'd been about not being accepted, I had never planned on going anywhere else next year.

And to be told I'd been *accepted* but then denied because of something completely out of my control, a total fluke in the system, a twist of fate....That was the worst part. *I had it.* I had made it to the finish line only to be stripped of my trophy.

What was I going to do now? Was I strong enough to get through all of this? Was I actually going to go to Clover Community College next year and spend more time fighting the same fight? Or was I just going to throw in the towel and give up, maybe join Mom on the couch?

I felt my cell phone buzz in my pocket. I had a voice mail from Mom—several, actually. I must have not noticed she was trying to call me.

"Carson, Grandma fell. Try to get over here as soon as you can," she said, obviously not knowing how to handle the situation on her own.

Maybe that's why this whole thing was happening? I was never supposed to leave Clover. The whole purpose of my existence was to take care of Mom and Grandma.

I got to the home as quickly as I could. Grandma was asleep when I got there. Her forearm was badly bruised, but other than that she seemed to be okay.

"Where were you?" Mom asked me as soon as I walked in. I didn't answer her. Where did she *think* I had been? "Fine, don't tell me, but if you were at your father's, I would be okay with it," she said.

"How is she?" I asked.

"Fine," Mom said. "Besides her arm, she bruised her hip, but nothing is broken. I'm going to get some coffee. Do you want anything?"

"No," I said, and Mom left Grandma's room.

Grandma slowly woke up a minute or so later. She looked up at me, and for a split second, I swear she recognized my face. She was quickly distracted by her injuries and the connection was lost.

"What happened to me?" she asked, looking at the bruise on her arm.

"You fell and hurt yourself," I said.

She looked back up at me. This time I was certain she knew who I was.

"You remind me of my grandson," she said to me. It was the closest she had been to lucid in years.

"I do?" I asked her happily. "Why is that?"

"You're sad-looking," she said. "My grandson used to be such a happy boy. He used to write me stories. I remember the first story he ever wrote me, '*Once upon a time, there was a boy.*' And that became '*Once upon a time there was a boy who wanted to fly.*' And they kept getting better and better over time. I never found out if the boy got to fly."

I gave her a small smile. If only she knew the boy's wings had been clipped.

Later the nurses came in to give Grandma a sponge bath. I went outside and found Mom on a bench. She seemed a bit overwhelmed by the whole thing, but I wasn't sure what part was stressing her out more: the fact that her mother had injured herself or that she actually had to get dressed and leave the house.

"What's going on?" Mom asked.

"They're giving her a bath," I said, and sat down next to her. She could tell something was wrong with me, but I wasn't exactly hiding behind a smile.

"What's your problem?" she asked me.

I was hesitant to tell her at first. I was still secretly hoping this day had just been a nightmare.

"I got into Northwestern, but I never got a letter, so now I have to wait to reapply," I said with a heavy heart.

A silence fell between us. I figured she was just disappointed to hear the news like I was but couldn't form the words to tell me how sorry she was. I couldn't have been more mistaken.

"I threw your letter away," Mom said quietly.

I swear my heart skipped a beat. I forgot where I was. I forgot we were outside. I forgot all about Grandma hurting herself. All I could think about was what my own mother had just confessed to me.

"What?!" I said.

"I'm sorry," she said.

"How could you— How could you throw my letter away?!" I said.

"I wanted to protect you," Mom said.

"Protect me?!" I said.

"I didn't want you to get hurt like I did," she said. "All your talk about growing up and becoming a writer—all these delusions you have won't happen. Dreams don't come true, Carson, take it from me. I'm living proof. The world is a very cruel place. You would have left and been eaten alive and come back utterly destroyed. I wanted better for you."

I couldn't believe it. My own mother, my own flesh and blood, had done this to me, and now she was trying to *validate* her actions.

"I can't believe this. This is so unfair!" I said, practically blind with anger.

"*Life* is unfair," Mom said. "It is. And the sooner you realize that, the faster you grow up and see the world for what it really is."

I stood up and walked away from her. In that moment, she was the most pathetic person in the world to me, and I couldn't stand being near her for another second.

"Thank you," I said to her. "Thank you for being the *perfect* example of something I refuse to become."

I got in my car and just drove. I drove and I drove and I drove. I wasn't sure where I was going and I didn't care. I didn't even plan on coming back, to be totally honest.

I passed the CLOVER CITY LIMIT sign on the outskirts

of town. It ignited a fire inside of me. I reached for my umbrella in the backseat, got out of my car with the engine still on, and went at that sign like a piñata.

I beat that sign until my fingernails bled and my umbrella was broken to pieces. I left a dent in it for every asshole who had treated me like shit, for every time I had been used, and for every time I had been wronged. But there wasn't any candy scattered across the ground, only fragments and broken pieces of the dream inside of me.

I tossed my ruined umbrella to the side of the road and got back in my car. I drove some more. This time I didn't stop for hours. I drove as far as I could until there was no more road left to take.

I found myself at the ocean. I sat on the hood of my car and just took in the sight of it. It was so beautiful. It seemed so endless and everlasting, just like how I used to feel.

The sun slowly set and night started to fall. I almost felt betrayed in a way, knowing the sun would rise again the next day. How could life continue after a day like this?

The last couple of days have been really hard, the hardest I've ever had to experience. Every morning I wake up I'm a little surprised. I sort of thought my heart would just stop beating while I slept. Is it possible to die from heartbreak or disappointment at my age?

I haven't been able to speak to Mom, or really look at her even. But could you? She keeps trying to apologize and tell me how sorry she is, but I really can't bear to listen to her.

I went into Ms. Sharpton's office and filled out a Clover Community College application. She gave me the most awkward hug after I did. You know your life sucks when the triple-divorcée beauty-school flunk-out feels sorry for you.

Ironically, we've been having really bad weather lately. It's been cloudy all week, so even the sky is a reminder of my state of mind.

I have every right to feel depressed and miserable, but I've been doing a lot of thinking this afternoon and have kind of developed a new perspective on things.

It started when Malerie met me here in the journalism classroom a couple of hours ago.

We packed up all the unsold (so all the) copies of the literary magazine and put them in boxes.

"What are we going to do with all these?" Malerie asked.

"I'm donating them to my grandmother's home," I said. "Someone is coming here later to pick them up. At least they'll be read…or chewed."

"I'm so sorry things didn't work out the way you wanted them to," Malerie said sweetly.

"Me too," I said. "But it looks like I'll be seeing you around Clover Community College next year. Maybe we'll be adventurous and start a literary magazine there?"

Malerie smiled at the idea but the thought really saddened me. Was that the best thing I could come up with to look forward to?

It was getting late and Malerie collected all of her stuff, including her camcorder. She had set it on a table, where it had been filming us pack the entire afternoon.

"Malerie, why do you film everything?" I asked her,

as I had been meaning to for a long time. "I mean, do you really want to remember *everything*?"

Malerie looked to the ceiling like she always does when someone asks her a *why do you do that?* question.

"What isn't worth remembering?" Malerie asked. "With good memories come bad memories, and I've got a lot of both. At least this way I can fast-forward through all the bad stuff."

I nodded to myself. She had a point.

"A counselor told me once that it doesn't matter if you are stuck in the past or trying to forget the past; what matters is what you do with the present. So that's why I try to soak it up as much as possible," she said.

"Malerie, I think you just found something to *write* about," I said with a smile. Malerie's eyes lit up with excitement and she smiled the biggest smile I've ever seen her have at the thought of writing her first original story.

"I've got to go," Malerie said. "If I'm late for the bus the driver said he'll make me ride in the trunk—it's not fun." Just before she got to the door she turned back to me. "Carson?" she asked with difficulty. "Are we *friends*?"

I was a little amused and heartbroken at the same time by the question. Did she really have to ask?

"I think we're best friends, Malerie," I said.

She shot me a gangster sign and left the classroom. I laughed for the first time in days.

I always knew Malerie had had a rough life, but I've never once asked her about it. Maybe something good will come out of my extended stay in Clover. Maybe I can finally be as good a friend to Malerie as she's always been to me. I guess I was so busy trying to get people to hear me, I never thought about listening.

I had one more box of magazines to pack for Grandma's home. Before I taped the box shut, I picked up a copy and flipped through the pages. For the first time since I completed it, I felt a strong sense of pride at seeing all the work of my peers in my hands and knowing I'd inspired it—illegally, of course, but I had influenced it nonetheless.

I smiled to myself and shook my head. Perhaps I've been so busy dwelling in my own sorrow I forgot about what I actually accomplished? I successfully published a literary magazine filled with the thoughts, concerns, hopes, and dreams of my jaded high school peers.

If I can do *that*, surely I can do anything, right? It's proof that the sky is the limit.

"The sky . . ." I said to myself. I immediately jumped behind my computer and began typing. I had one more story to add to the magazine.

I printed out copies of the story once I was finished. I opened all the boxes and put the new story in the front of every copy of the literary magazine. It also acted as a dedication of sorts:

To Grandma:
Once upon a time,
there was a boy who *flew*.

I don't think the magazine could have started any better. And seeing that in the front of my magazine gave me a feeling I'm not sure I've ever felt before; I think it made me *happy*.

Yes, unfortunately we live in a world where the pretty, the popular, and the wealthy sometimes prevail over the rest. And yes, sometimes people and circumstances get in the way of achieving your dreams and seeing your visions all the way through. And yes, if you hold an advantage over everyone else while you're out there trying to get there (intelligence, creativity, or drive), people will always try to bring you down that much more.

But if I let *those* types of people bring me down, the people too pigheaded to encourage the good I'm trying to spread in the world, then I'm not as smart as I think I am.

From this day on, I refuse to let anyone bring me to a point where I can't take a horrible situation and spin it into *something* beneficial. I will never let anyone make me feel anything I don't want to feel again or rob me of the passions that make me who I am.

Does it suck ass that I have to spend another two years in a town full of people who hate my guts? Absolutely. Am I going to hate every minute of it? Probably. But I'm also entering a brand-new campus with absolutely nothing to lose and no friends to make.

Hell hath no fury like a journalist with nothing to lose. Just imagine the editorials I'll have to submit to Northwestern the next time I apply!

Even if I never get out of Clover, even if I never get into Northwestern or write for the *New Yorker*, even if these are just delusions occupying my time, thank God they are, because a life without meaning, without drive or focus, without dreams or goals, isn't a life worth living.

And after learning that, I may have made the greatest realization of my young life, and it reminds me of that conversation I had with Malerie all those months ago.

Like having a great idea, *life* comes at you fast. It hits you and tries to escape and be expressed in any way possible. In a way, it's a lot like...*lightning*.

Speaking of which, I think I hear a storm coming. I should head home before it starts to rain; I seem to have misplaced my umbrella.

CHS STUDENT KILLED, STRUCK BY LIGHTNING

ERICA PLOTKIN

March 16, 2013

CLOVER, CALIFORNIA—The body of Clover High School senior Carson Phillips was discovered in the student parking lot the morning of Friday, March 16. According to the coroner's report, Phillips was killed when he was struck by a bolt of lightning during the storm in the late afternoon of Thursday, March 15.

"I think I speak on behalf of all the students and faculty when I say Carson was an absolute joy and he will be missed," Clover High principal Barry Gifford said in a statement to the local press. "There wasn't a single person on campus who didn't love the guy."

"We were best friends," said fellow senior Remy Baker. "It's so sad to think we won't see him walking through the halls anymore."

Although no one in Phillips's family cared to comment on the tragic passing, after many attempts by local reporters the deceased's mother, Sheryl, finally had this to say: "I was reading that lightning is a negative charge that comes from the friction clouds carry. Since opposites attract, I would like to think that he was so positive the moment he died—so happy, he pulled that bolt right out of the sky. I don't know if that's possible, but that's what I believe."

A service will be held this Sunday at the Clover Community Chapel. In lieu of flowers, the family has asked that donations be made to the Clover High Writers' Club.

Acknowledgments

I'd like to thank Rob, Monica, and the entire Aguirre family. Without them, *Struck By Lightning* would still be a screenplay on my shelf.

I'd also like to thank:

Brian Dannelly, David Permut, Steve Longi, Jason Berman, Mia Chang, Lawrence Kopeikin, Mark Moran, Chris Mangano, and Romy Rosemont.

The incredible cast of the film, including Allison Janney, Christina Hendricks, Dermot Mulroney, Rebel Wilson, Polly Bergen (I love you, honey!), Angela Kinsey, Sarah Hyland, Robbie Amell, Ashley Rickards, Allie Grant (Allie, I think you're beautiful, sorry Carson hates Remy so much!), Matt Prokop, Carter Jenkins, Graham Rogers, Charlie Finn, Brad William Henke, Ginifer King, Adam Kolkin, Luke Lewis, Lauren Lopez, and Amy Nabors.

Bobby Bukowski, Bridgette Kelley (my spirit animal!), Wendy Chuck, Linda Burton, Tia Nolan, Kyle Burch, Drew Ann Rosenberg, Christopher Wolfe, Aaron Penn, Denise Paulson, Brian Steven Banks, Heidi Hanson, Suzanne Houchin, and the rest of the spectacular *SBL* crew.

The Little, Brown team, including Alvina Ling, Bethany Strout, Megan Tingley, Andrew Smith, and Melanie Chang, and everyone at Tribeca Film.

Last but certainly not least, the members of my own team, Rob Weisbach, Alla Plotkin, Erica Tarin, Meredith Fine, Derek Kroeger, Heather Manzutto, and Elizabeth Uhl. And a very special thanks to Glenn Rigberg, the biggest *SBL* champion, who made it all happen.

Also, Oprah, Madonna, Queen Elizabeth, Jennifer Saunders, and Woody Allen…because I can.

Permut Presentations and Camellia Entertainment
In Association with **Inphenate**
Presents **A film by** Brian Dannelly
Chris Colfer Allison Janney **STRUCK BY LIGHTNING** Christina Hendricks
Sarah Hyland Carter Jenkins Brad William Henke Rebel Wilson Angela Kinsey
with Polly Bergen **and** Dermot Mulroney
Casting by Anya Colloff & Michael Nicolo **Score Produced by** Christophe Beck
Original Score by Jake Monaco **Costume Designer** Wendy Chuck
Production Designer Linda Burton **Edited by** Tia Nolan
Director of Photography Bobby Bukowski **Co-Producers** Monica Aguirre Diez Barroso Steve Longi Mark Moran
Executive Producers Jason Michael Berman Chris Colfer Glenn Rigberg Lawrence Kopeikin
Produced by David Permut Roberto Aguire Mia Chang
Written by Chris Colfer **Directed by** Brian Dannelly

GO TO THE CORNER OF NOTHING AND NOWHERE, MAKE A LEFT....

The Clover High
Chronicle

Editor
Caren Philips

D.N.A.
DEFINITELY NOT ADOPTED.

SMART IS
THE NEW
SEXY!

WORST COUNSELOR EVER!

DON'T SCOTT, DON'T TELL

"DESENSITIZED" DWAYNE

SELF-RIGHTEOUS REMY

CONTRACEPTION CLAIRE

IMPORTED EMILIO

JUSTIN, THE THIRD TWEEDLE

VIP VICKI (VAMPIRE IN PROGRESS)

PRINCE NICHOLAS OF TRUSTFUNDOM (THAT MEANS HE'S RICH!)

ASS EMBLY!

HOMECOMING
BLOWS!

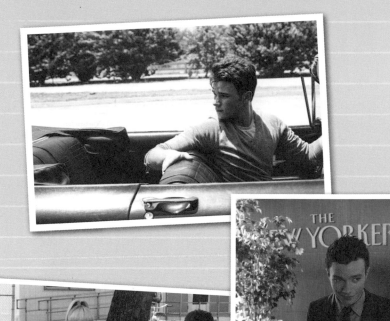

THE
DREAM!

PARTNERS IN CRIME.

SOMETIMES A PERSONAL RAIN CLOUD CAN BE DEADLY.